Jaguar Island 3

The Jaguar's Secret Baby

BIANCA D'ARC

Copyright © 2019 Bianca D'Arc
Published by Hawk Publishing, LLC

Hank has never forgotten the wild woman with whom he spent one memorable night. He's dreamed of her for years, but has never been back to the small airport in Texas owned and run by her werewolf Pack. Tracy was left with a delicious memory of her night in Hank's arms, and a beautiful baby girl who is the light of her life. She chose not to tell Hank about his daughter, but when he finally returns and he discovers the daughter he's never known, he'll do all he can to set things right.

Tracy wants to be wanted for herself and won't settle for less. Hank realizes he's been a stupid fool and the woman he's never been able to forget is actually his mate. He's just been too stubborn to admit it. He will need to prove his devotion before his werewolf mate will relent and give in to the attraction that has never faded. He just needs to find the right words and actions to make her understand and win her heart all over again.

* This book is the third in the Jaguar Island series, which is also part of the larger Tales of the Were series. Jaguar Island contains:
1. The Jaguar Tycoon
2. The Jaguar Bodyguard
3. The Jaguar's Secret Baby

DEDICATION

With much love for my readers, especially Mary Worley who gave me some information about super glue being used to seal wounds when our discussions on social media led into strange waters. I put a scene in this book (you'll know which one I mean when you read it) because of that conversation. Just goes to show...I never quite know where ideas are going to come from!

And the inspiration for that entire conversation deserves a mention—my dear old Dad, who is on two different blood thinners and was bleeding a lot from a very small cut when I posted to social media, seeking information. I didn't use super glue on him, but I did get a lot of good pointers from the hive mind, which was greatly appreciated. Thanks to you all.

PROLOGUE

"Who is the father?" Tracy's father demanded.

He might be Alpha of the Big Wolf Pack, and therefore the owner of Big Wolf Airport, Big Wolf Barbeque, where she worked, and mayor of Big Wolf, Texas, but she was his daughter, and he couldn't really compel her with his dominance. They were too much alike. She was a dominant female in her own right, and she'd long ago, grown accustomed to her father's bark. He would never bite one of his own over something like this, so she knew she was safe, which gave her added strength to deny his command.

"I'm still not telling you, Dad. Now, if you want your first grandchild to be born without medical assistance, just keep doing what you're doing. Otherwise, I came downstairs to call the midwife." She made her way slowly toward the phone.

She should've had her cell phone by her bed, but she hadn't been thinking clearly these last nine months. Doing stupid stuff had become the norm ever since she'd discovered she was pregnant. Pregnant and unmated. At her age. As the result of a one-night stand. Could she get any more pathetic?

Okay, it had been the best one-nighter of her life, but still... Pregnancy shouldn't have been the result. He wasn't even a wolf! It shouldn't have been possible to be so damned fertile across species like this, but the little person clamoring

1

to get out had other ideas.

"You mean it's coming, now?" Her father's face paled.

She would have laughed if a contraction hadn't hit her just at that moment. She leaned against the kitchen island and grit her teeth as she growled low in her throat through the pain. That seemed to set her dad in motion. He grabbed the phone and dialed the number for the Pack's healer. She heard the conversation in the background as the pain stole her breath and made her want to howl. The important thing was, her father was getting help. When the pain eased, he was at her side, loving concern on his face.

"They're on their way," he told her in a soothing tone. "Now, can you walk, or should I carry you back to your room? I assume that's where you want this to happen, right?"

She nodded and leaned heavily on him as they went out of the kitchen together, but the staircase was beyond her. Her steps faltered, and her father picked her up, as he had when she was little, and mounted the stairs with her in his arms. He didn't put her down until they had reached her bed. He deposited her gently on the bed she had prepared. It was covered in toweling with plastic underneath so she wouldn't ruin the mattress.

Aida had helped her gather the necessary supplies and would—Goddess willing—see her through this birth. Aida was the midwife, mated to the Pack's healer, Giuseppe. They were both on the way here, according to her dad, but she really only needed Aida. They'd been talking about this for almost nine months—ever since Tracy realized she was pregnant—and they'd been making plans the whole time.

Aida was the mother Tracy no longer had, and she probably couldn't have handled this situation half as well without her guidance. Aida had been close to Tracy's mother and had stepped in to help when Tracy's mom had died in a terrible accident. Tracy still missed her vibrant, vivacious mother every day, but it was good to have someone like Aida around to help.

Tracy's father didn't leave her side, looking around to see

what he could do to help prepare, but there wasn't anything. She'd done it all last week and had only been waiting for the signal that the little one was ready to meet the world. It felt like it wouldn't be long now.

"Tracy, sweetheart," her father said, sitting at her side and pushing her hair back from her brow. "Who did this? Who's the father?"

Stubborn Alpha wolf. Tracy smiled. "Why? So you can go hunt him down and shanghai him into mating with me? Dad, this isn't 1850 anymore." She named the year her father had been born and rolled her eyes.

"A man should be there for his children," he insisted. "At the very least, he should help support the pup."

"I don't need his money." She shook her head. "And I don't need his interference."

Dawning realization broke over her father's face. "Sweet Mother of All. You haven't even told him!"

Tracy grimaced. She'd debated a long time over whether it was better to let her father think poorly of her child's father or reveal that she hadn't tracked down the perpetrator and told him about the impending birth. She'd just let it ride, not really knowing what to do, and hoping a path would reveal itself. Well, it looked like the revelation had just taken place, and she wasn't altogether sure it was a good thing. Now, it was solidly her fault that the baby's father wasn't here. Tracy felt a little guilty, but really…it was an impossible situation.

"Is he even a wolf?" her father asked, his tone aghast. He'd been eyeing every male in the Pack with suspicion for the past few months, but it hadn't done him any good. The father wasn't a Pack member. "Is he even a shifter?"

She could give him that much, she figured. "Yes, he's a shifter, but no, he's not one of ours. And that's all I have to say on the matter." She gasped as another pain hit and grabbed her father's hand.

He didn't say anything more until the contraction had passed.

"I'll accept that," he told her, his eyes narrowing, and his dominance a palpable thing in the room. "For now."

Tracy gulped, but Aida bustled into the room and shooed Tracy's father out. Giuseppe was waiting in the hallway, and Tracy saw him put a friendly arm around her father's shoulders before guiding him away from the bedroom. Giuseppe would keep her father distracted while the women got down to business.

Goddess help them all.

CHAPTER 1

Two years later…

Heinrich Schleichender—Hank, to his American friends—
started his final descent into Big Wolf Airport in Texas. He
hadn't been able to come back this way for far too long. The
fact that he'd been given a mission by his Alpha that would
take him through this part of the world for the next few
weeks, perhaps months, made his beast half's fur ripple with
satisfaction.

He'd been trying to get back to Texas for the past two or
three years, but circumstances had been against him. With the
rise of the Venifucus—an evil order of mages intent on
destruction—Hank had been called on, time and time again,
by his friend and Alpha, Mark Pepard, to spearhead
investigations and negotiations all over the world.

That Hank was multi-lingual, one of the top pilots in the
Clan, and a trusted associate of the leadership meant he was
much in demand. When a delicate touch was called for to set
up sensitive deals, Hank was the go-to guy. Clan business had
kept him busy. So busy, in fact, that he hadn't been able to
get back to Texas at all…until now.

Hank had never been able to forget the woman he'd met
here in Big Wolf, Texas—Tracy. The Alpha wolf's daughter.

They'd spent one passionate night together before duty to his Clan had called him away. Things had been in an uproar for a while in the Jaguar Clan led by billionaire Mark Pepard. Hank had spent most of the last few years flying special missions for Mark, on behalf of the Clan.

This mission, in fact, was another one of those special tasks set for Hank by the Alpha. He was to open negotiations with a small jaguar Clan based in Arizona, inviting them to take their place in the larger group that was centralizing operations on Jaguar Island. Of special interest were two of the stronger Alphas in the Arizona group—a pair of fraternal twins who had Special Forces backgrounds and were currently working freelance as mercenaries.

Mark wanted their skills, and he wanted all the jaguars to know they had a place on the island, if they wanted it. He'd been slowly reaching out to the family groups and Clans that remained after urbanization and drug wars had killed far too many of their people. Mark had bought the island and secured it. Now, he was bringing in more jaguars to make their homes there—safe from the dangers of the human world, while the Clan rebuilt its decimated numbers.

They could use more men with skills like Pax and Ari Rojas, along with the rest of their Clan members in Arizona. It was one of the larger groups, but it still wasn't huge. They, too, had felt the impact of the drug wars that took out so many of their people.

As the drug cartels took over vast stretches of jungle, they pushed out the jaguars who had lived there. At some point, with nowhere left to retreat, the jaguars tried to fight back, but their solitary lifestyles and the need for territory of their own had left them all too vulnerable. No matter how strong a particular shifter or family group was, once a sufficiently large number of humans with automatic weapons arrived, they didn't really stand a chance.

The story had repeated itself all over South America for decades. Some survivors regrouped in the United States. Some had been in the States all along. The Arizona group was a mix of native and immigrant populations, and it was Hank's task to make it clear that all jaguars who served the Light were welcome on Jaguar Island. Negotiations would be tricky, though. Cats were generally solitary and territorial. Any family group that had stuck together the way the Arizona Clan had usually had large stretches of territory for each family member, so nobody felt crowded. The Arizona Clan was of particular interest to Mark Pepard and the larger Jaguar Clan, though, because of those two soldier-of-fortune brothers. Their skills and connections could come in very useful, if they could be persuaded to work for the good of the Jaguar people as a whole.

Which was Hank's mission. It might take multiple trips out to Arizona. Everyone knew cats were fickle, and it sometimes took a bit of time to convince them to do what you wanted them to do. Nobody knew that better than another jaguar. Hank had been chosen because he had Mark's confidence, trust, and was known to be a careful, patient predator when he was on the stalk.

Pax and Ari Rojas might not realize it, but they were most definitely being stalked...for the good of their species.

"Clear for landing," came the instruction from the Big Wolf Airport tower over Hank's headset.

He was on approach, and it wouldn't be long before he set down and taxied to his assigned parking space. Then, he'd arrange for refueling and stop for some lunch at the famous Big Wolf Barbeque restaurant near the airport. He couldn't wait to get on the ground and see if maybe Tracy was around.

He would try to be casual, but the way his inner jaguar was sitting up in eagerness of the hunt was something he suddenly found hard to control. His inner beast had never forgotten the pretty wolf woman, strange as that seemed. His cat admired her and wanted to play with her wolf form. Run and stalk, roll in the tall grass. Hank shook his head. His cat had never found a playmate outside their own species before, but then again, his cat side was a lot more playful than most.

His Clan mates teased him about the way his cat form was

always ready to play. It wasn't the norm for solitary cats, but it fit Hank's unusually positive personality. His family had gone through a lot of dark stuff in the past. Perhaps Hank's sunny outlook was a result of that. He couldn't be sure. He hadn't been alive for the wrong turns taken by some of his ancestors, but he'd decided early on that he could either live his life feeling ashamed of the decisions they'd made or forge a new path for himself, firmly on the side of Light.

He'd chosen the latter, and after initial hesitation, Mark Pepard had accepted him into the Clan. Hank had proven himself, over and over again, until the last of Mark's doubts had been erased. Hank had the approval and confidence of the highest ranks in the Clan. Anything others might still say about his ancestors might sting, but he knew who he was, and he wasn't like them at all. Not one bit.

With a few more radio transmissions and a bit of maneuvering, Hank was on the ground at last. He parked the small plane where instructed and grabbed his duffel bag. He had come prepared to bribe Tracy's little brother with the latest video game, if necessary. If not, he'd still give the kid the early release version everyone was clamoring for—that Hank had gotten before release through his contacts. Kevin was a good kid. He deserved a treat, even if it turned out he wouldn't help Hank stalk his sister.

But Hank had an idea where she might be. The whole family worked either at the airport or the restaurant. Their father was the Alpha and owner of the two very successful businesses, as well as being the mayor of the town the Pack had built around itself. The Big Wolf Pack was employed in all the Pack businesses, particularly the Alpha's family and inner circle, who tended to run things. Last time Hank had checked—only a week ago—Tracy had been the general manager of the restaurant. It was likely she'd be there, since it was around lunchtime on a weekday. The place would be busy, but maybe she'd take a few minutes to talk to him.

That goal firmly in mind, Hank headed out of the airport and over to the restaurant.

*

"Em, honey, come back here," Tracy called after her adventurous daughter, who was running off, yet again, pushing through the forest of people's legs, in the front lobby of the restaurant. It was one of her favorite games, and the Pack indulged her a little too much, in Tracy's opinion.

Emma's little blonde pigtails bounced as she made her way forward. She was an adorable baby. Fair skinned and with dark blonde hair that was a mix of her mother's chestnut and her father's golden blond. But, only Tracy knew that little secret. Nobody in the Pack knew who or what Emma's father was, or what he looked like. Just Tracy.

Emma was out of sight, and Tracy sped up to catch her wayward two year old. She spotted Em, stopped against the legs of a man, clinging to the poor fellow like a burr. Thankfully, everyone present was Pack. At least, Tracy thought they were all shifters, if not all members of her Pack. Though…there was a tantalizing new scent at the edge of her perception.

With all the wolves waiting to be seated—a party of fourteen had just come in from the airport and wanted to sit together—it was hard to discern the new shifter scent, but as Tracy drew nearer to her daughter, the scent became sharper. It was familiar, somehow, and her inner wolf sat up from her lazy doze in Tracy's mind and started to look around through Tracy's eyes. Something was…

Sweet Mother of All.

The Pack members parted before her, clearing a path to her daughter, clinging to a man Tracy hadn't seen in more than two years. Closer to three, actually.

Hank. The golden-haired sex god Tracy had never forgotten.

Her baby's father.

The baby he didn't know about.

Hank looked up, a happy smile on his face that he'd been

giving her daughter when the crowd hushed. Their eyes met, and his smile got even bigger. He was pleased to see her, but would he be so pleased once he realized she was a mother and not free to play with him the way she had years ago?

She gritted her teeth against what had to be done. "Emma, honey, let the nice man go and come to Mama." She bent down to catch the little scamp, who abandoned her new friend as soon as her mother caught up with her.

Emma tucked up close to her heart, Tracy looked up to meet Hank's sky-blue gaze. He looked crestfallen for a split second before he pasted a congenial expression on his face.

"Hi, Tracy," he said, his deep voice hitting down deep in the place where her wolf howled in welcome. "Long time, no see."

"Hello, Hank." She couldn't say anything else. Emotion nearly choked her as she stood, lifting her baby girl in her arms.

Emma was getting big, but Tracy was a wolf. She could easily carry Emma, who clung to her neck, though she turned her head to look Hank. Her big blue eyes watched him curiously.

"She's yours," Hank said, unnecessarily. "Congratulations on…your mating," he finished somewhat lamely. Tracy didn't hear joy in his words. Or, maybe, she was reading too much into his tone. Maybe she was hearing what she longed to hear.

He was still so tall and muscular, her mouth went dry at the sight of him. His hair was a little longer than it had been all those years ago, but that was about the only change she really noticed. He was still just as handsome and just as much a draw to her starved senses as he had been during their first encounter.

"I'm not mated," she revealed on a deep breath. "But I do have the love of my life, as you see." She bent to kiss Emma's soft cheek, and the child giggled, the sound filling the empty places in Tracy's heart, as it always did.

Hank looked confused, but he hid it after a second.

"I was wondering, if you haven't already eaten, would

you—and your daughter—like to have lunch with me?"

Brave man to ask her to share a meal in a lobby filled with her Pack mates. They all knew he was a cat. He smelled feline…and ferocious, she'd always thought. Forbidden. Cats and dogs didn't mix. At least according to her father. But she'd liked the way she and Hank had mixed during their stolen night together. She'd liked it a lot.

And the little girl wriggling in her arms was proof of that. Tracy opened her mouth to answer his question when a wave of shifter magic caught her unawares…

Hank was caught completely flat-footed by the gorgeous baby girl in Tracy's arms. She was a joyful child, and the mischief in her baby blue eyes spoke to something in his own soul. He'd been charmed when the little beauty accosted him in the crowd, but then, his emotions had swung into chaos when he realized the child was Tracy's. If Tracy had found her mate and started a family, then any hope he had of renewing their relationship had just gone up in flames.

Then, his emotions had been tugged in the other direction at her claim that she was still unmated, though she was a single mother. He admired the strength in her voice as she spoke her truth. Tracy had always been a powerful woman, and he'd enjoyed coaxing her into playing with him. They were both strong shifters, but together, they didn't have to compete for dominance. They could just…be. Together.

It had been wonderful while it lasted. An all-too-brief affair. He'd tried for the past two years and more to get back to her, but his duties to his Alpha had kept him far away.

Somehow, he had dug up the nerve to ask her to have lunch with him. He wanted to know everything that had happened in her life since they'd last met. He wanted to know where the child's father was, and if he was still in the picture. He wanted, more than anything, to have some place in Tracy's—and now Emma's—life. As much of a place as she'd let him have.

He was waiting for her answer when a magical wave

reached out to him. The child... The child was emitting shifter magic in a familiar pattern he had experienced a few times on Jaguar Island, now that Mark had gathered their people together and there were little baby jaguars running around the place.

But Hank had always thought wolves were different. They didn't usually start shifting until they hit puberty. Didn't they? And yet... There was no denying the magic coming from the little girl now struggling in her mother's arms. She wanted to be put down, and even before Tracy had released the girl completely, a golden shimmer enveloped the child.

Clothes fell away, and a little furry body lay within the drape of the child's dress. It struggled its way out, the entire crowd in the busy lobby now watching in silence, waiting to see how she would emerge. Something significant was going on here, but Hank barely registered their surroundings, except to note that nobody seemed intent on harming the girl or interfering with her shift. He read the crowd as curious. Maybe overly so. But not dangerous.

Then, the little girl's head emerged from under the fabric and...she was golden with little black spots. She was...

Sweet Mother of All! She was a jaguar.

CHAPTER 2

Tracy watched Hank bend down to extend his arms to the little fur ball that was her daughter. Emma ran to him, unsteady on her paws but seemingly happy to seek the comfort of Hank's embrace. Hank stood, cradling their daughter expertly, allowing Emma to curl up in his big hands. She was such a tiny cat. No bigger than a housecat. In fact, she was smaller than most housecats, but Tracy knew Emma would grow into something a lot bigger.

Hank stroked Emma's head, scratching behind her little tufted ears. She really was the most adorable thing in her fur, though this was the very first time Tracy had seen it. She hadn't been prepared for this. Wolf children didn't start shifting for years yet! Was it her father's presence that had sparked Emma's first shift?

Fate had a funny way of making Tracy admit to the man she'd spent one glorious night with that he was a daddy. She'd been so afraid when she first found out she was pregnant. Fear of how Hank would react, how her father and Pack would take the news, and what would happen if they learned her baby's father wasn't even a wolf, but a jaguar, of all things, had kept her quiet. Over time, it had just been easier to keep her secret, even after Emma was born.

She'd agonized over whether to try to contact Hank. He

hadn't exactly left a forwarding address when he'd flown away. She could try his Clan, but then, she'd have to involve even more people in what should be a private matter. They'd probably want to know why she was so keen to find him, and how could she explain that she'd gotten knocked up after such a brief encounter? It still didn't seem possible. Cross-species sex wasn't supposed to be all that fertile, even when the two parties were mates.

Then, once Emma was born, the fear had changed to what Hank might do when he found out about his child. Would he try to take her away? Would he interfere in how Tracy was raising her daughter? Would he be murdered by her father when Dad discovered the truth? Or worse—would either of them try to make her marry Hank, or something equally stupid?

Realistically, she and Hank barely knew each other, except in the rawest, most physical ways. Their encounter had been about sex and need and attraction. It had also been fun. Hank was a great guy to be around. He had a joyful, playful nature that was very attractive. But their night together hadn't been meant to last forever. Not even close. And yet…Emma was the result, and that little baby had stolen Tracy's heart forevermore. If it had been up to her, Tracy probably would've kept Emma all to herself for as long as possible.

But the cat was—quite literally—out of the bag.

"Uh, Tracy? Is there something you maybe wanted to tell me?"

Hank's expression was a mix of both delight and astonishment, with more than a bit of anger around the edges. Yeah, she knew he had a right to be angry with her, but she was glad to see that, so far, he wasn't taking it out on Em.

"Yeah," Tracy admitted, one hand reaching up to massage the tight muscles at the back of her neck in reflex. "I suppose so."

She became very aware suddenly that they were not alone. Far from it. Half the Pack was in the lobby, witnessing one of the most embarrassing and potentially pivotal moments of her life. *Damn.*

"Come with me, Hank," she said, leading him toward the back, where the offices were located. Maybe they could get a little privacy, after the fact, for the conversation that needed to happen, now.

She wanted to reach out and take Emma from his arms but curbed the impulse. Em was safe with Hank. Tracy knew that on a basic level that went beyond instinct. Hank would protect her—any child, really—with his life. He was one of the good guys.

Hank was totally astonished at the turn of events. He'd finally returned to Texas, hoping to spend more time with the woman he'd never been able to forget, only to find…this. The most adorable little kitten, who scented of family.

Hank had no doubt in his mind that little Em was his daughter. His and Tracy's little girl, born of the one night of passion they had shared. It almost beggared belief. Shifters were notoriously hard to impregnate unless the blessing of the Goddess was upon the union.

Mates were fertile with each other. Other joinings? Not so much.

In fact, it was almost unheard of to have a child with someone who was not your mate. And that held true for most shifter species. Jaguars and wolves, too, as far as Hank knew. So, then. Where had little Emma come from? And what did this mean for her erstwhile parents?

Was there a deeper reason why Hank had never seemed able to get Tracy out of his mind? Was she the real reason he hadn't given much thought to sex in the years since they'd parted? He'd thought his long dry spell was just due to overwork and lack of opportunity in the places he'd been sent by the Clan. But maybe there was more to it. Maybe he hadn't been interested in other liaisons because there really was only one woman for him, and he'd found her without really trying.

Could he be that stupid that he hadn't recognized the

signs? Could he have been in denial all this time that Tracy was his destined mate? Hank had to shake his head. He just didn't know.

That there was something special—something unforgettable—about her, he knew. But, somehow, he couldn't be certain they were mates. Not now. Not after only the one night so long ago. Maybe there was something wrong with his mating instincts. Or maybe it was harder to tell when the shifters involved weren't of the same species. Maybe his inner cat was confused about the idea of accepting a wolf into its life.

Hank had no way of knowing, but he sensed this mystery wasn't going to be solved right here and now. No, this would require a great deal of thought, a lot of analysis and perhaps even a bit of prayer.

In the meantime, there was this new little person to consider. Whatever he and Tracy decided about their own lives and involvement, they had to make sure what they chose to do was in Emma's best interests. She was the most important thing now.

But how in the world could Tracy not have told him? He was alternately astonished and mad as hell that she'd kept this from him for so long. And, if he hadn't shown up today, would she have kept his daughter's existence from him forever? Could she have been so cruel? He hadn't thought the woman he'd been with so long ago could be that mean, but then again, what did he really know about her deeper thoughts? Their relationship—if you could call it that—had been purely physical. Fun. Nothing serious. At least, not serious enough to have spawned the little furry beauty in his arms. Hank was probably in shock. His thoughts raced, and his anger came and went alongside his awe at the little girl's unexpected appearance in his life.

Tracy led him through a service corridor and into an office area. She didn't stop walking until they were in a private office. Her office, he realized, seeing the way it was set up and the items it contained. On the desk was a photo of herself with a younger Emma. Suddenly, Hank realized he'd missed quite a lot of Emma's life. A frown creased his brow as anger once again surged to the forefront of his mind.

Tracy turned to face him once the door was shut behind them. "Look, I'm sorry. I just didn't know how to tell you. Furthermore, I wasn't really sure how to contact you. I debated trying to track you down for a long time, but in the end, I didn't think it was right to burden you with a child you never intended to make."

Hank took a deep breath before replying. There were so many things wrong with what she'd just said, but he didn't want to let emotion take control. He was a skilled negotiator who often dealt with intense situations. When anger erupted, sense went out the window, and he didn't want that to happen here. Also, Emma was nearly asleep in his hands. He didn't want to wake her or worry her. She was innocent in all this. So, Hank moderated his tone as best he could.

"I may not have expected this to happen, but I had a right to know. Tracy..." He had to pause as emotion choked him. He cleared his throat and tried again. "Tracy. This little girl is a miracle. However she happened, clearly, I need to be a part of her life. She's a jaguar. How will she ever learn to be a cat if she's the only one in a Pack of wolves?"

"She's my daughter. My Pack wouldn't treat her badly. My family loves her and spoils her rotten already, even if my father asks if I've changed my mind about revealing who her father is every few weeks." Tracy rolled her eyes.

"They don't know?" Hank was surprised, but he supposed he shouldn't have been. If the Alpha of the Big Wolf Pack had known his granddaughter's parentage, Hank was fairly certain he would've been contacted long before now.

"Nobody knows," Tracy said, then seemed to think better of her words. "Well. Nobody *knew*. After this... I suppose word is spreading like wildfire through the Pack at this very moment."

She'd no sooner said the words than the office door opened and Tracy's father entered the room. He had an

Alpha-sized scowl on his face, and he looked about ready to bite Hank's face off if he said the slightest thing wrong. Hank brought Emma's sleeping form closer to his chest, ready to defend his child to the death, if that's what it took.

Tracy wanted to sink into the floor when her father showed up. Bad enough that her daughter's first shift happened in public, and in the presence of her totally unknowing father. Tracy was certain the gossip was all around the Pack by now, and her dad's arrival seemed to confirm it. No doubt some well-meaning busybody had phoned him first thing.

"Is this the father?" her father demanded. Tracy noticed the way Hank instinctually moved to protect their daughter.

"Dad…"

"Don't you stonewall me for another minute, missy!" her father thundered, waking Em, who started to shake in Hank's arms.

"I'll thank you to lower your voice, Alpha. Your granddaughter is growing alarmed at your tone." Hank's words were full of command, and Tracy had to wonder for the millionth time what Hank's position in his Clan was.

Was he an Alpha? He certainly felt powerful. But was he strong enough to stand up to the rigors of a very tight-knit werewolf Pack?

"It's true, then. Emma is a cat." The wolf Alpha imbued that last word with something akin to disgust, and Hank seemed to bristle.

"She's a jaguar, sir. Of a long and noble lineage. She's only…what? Two years old? And already shifting. If that doesn't speak of her power, just wait. You'll soon learn."

Tracy got chills down her spine when Hank spoke all formal like that. And his words hinted at things she'd been wondering about for the past two years. She really knew way too little about him.

"This was her first shift, actually," Tracy put in, looking at Hank.

"Your very first?" Hank lifted their daughter in his hands and looked into her eyes. He was smiling. "I'm so glad I was here to see it. You're a strong girl, aren't you?" The kitten reached out with one little paw and touched his cheek, almost petting him. Hank allowed it and snuggled Emma close. Tracy felt a little pang in the region of her heart. She was glad he'd been there, too. For a number of reasons. Not least of which was the fact that she wasn't really sure what to do with a baby jaguar shifter. All her experience was with her own kind, and they didn't generally start shifting until puberty. Totally different problems with adolescent shifters than with toddlers. Tracy would have to learn all about how to care for Em if she was going to be shifting so young.

Em turned to her and seemed to want to leap from Hank's arms into hers, but Hank caught her before she could try. He pinched the skin at her nape, and Emma quieted, going almost limp. Then, he lifted her and brought her over to Tracy, transferring their baby to her arms.

"Just like cats, when they are in this form, you can move them by the scruff of the neck without harm," Hank told her, concentrating on their child as he placed her securely into Tracy's arms. "It's helpful when both parent and child are in their fur. Instinct keeps them quiet while the parent transports them. It's a survival mechanism, I think."

Transfer complete, Hank stepped back a little, while Tracy marveled at the new form her daughter had taken. Never in Tracy's wildest dreams had she expected her baby to start shifting so young. Tracy had worried over what form Emma would take, considering her father was a jaguar, but Tracy had figured she had years yet.

Apparently not.

Before anybody could say anything else, a shower of magical energy burst from the kitten in Tracy's arms, and between one moment and the next, she went from holding a cat to holding her daughter in human form. She was naked, cute as a button, and rubbing her eyes with one fist.

"Tired, Mama," she said, and Tracy went into action.

She kept a little bed in her office for the days when her baby came to work with her—which was most of the time. She had a toddler-safe office, complete with play area and rest area for her baby. She set Emma down, put a quick diaper on her little butt, just in case, and pulled the covers over her. There would be time later to get her dressed. Em was probably tuckered out from her first shift and would sleep for a while. Then, she'd probably wake up hungry, to replace the energy she'd used in the effort of shifting. Tracy would be sure to have a meal ready and waiting when that happened, but for now, her baby needed sleep.

"Shall we go someplace else to talk?" Tracy asked, as politely as she could manage considering how much she dreaded the next few minutes. She picked up the baby monitor on her way out and preceded the men out the door.

They followed, and she led them to another office, just next door. It was the assistant manager's office. Her brother Ken's, actually. But Ken wasn't in today. He usually worked the night shift, leaving Tracy to deal with the daytime hours.

She took the strategic chair, behind Ken's desk. There were two visitor chairs, and the men took those. She was glad to have the wide desk between them, if only as a symbolic barrier. She expected her father to have a few things to say, and she didn't have to wait long to hear them.

"When, exactly, were you going to admit her father wasn't a wolf? You've been playing word games with me at every turn, keeping me guessing. I've been eyeing every non-Pack shifter I see—wolf or not—with suspicion for the past two years!" Her father's voice rose, making Tracy feel guilty.

"I'm sorry, Dad. I knew if I told you for sure that her father wasn't a wolf, you'd track down every non-wolf shifter who'd come through the airport or town in the right timeframe, and it wouldn't be long before you found Hank."

"Do you hate me that much?" Hank asked, his expression hard, but his tone bleak. Damn. This wasn't going well.

"No! Don't ever think that, Hank," she said quickly, trying

to fix what she'd done and knowing it was going to take time. She had to at least make a start right here and now. "I love our daughter, and I enjoyed my time with you, but I don't know enough about your life to know what you'd have done if you'd known about her from the beginning. I didn't want to give her up." She wanted him to understand, but she sensed it wasn't going to be easy.

"I would never have tried to take her from you. Never!" Hank replied, shocked. "A baby needs its mother." He settled those sky-blue eyes on her. "And its father."

She didn't have an answer to that.

"He's right, you know," her father said into the silence. "What you've done here wasn't right, Tracy. Not for any of you. Emma needs—especially now—her father."

Tracy shook her head. "I was hoping she'd be a wolf. I didn't expect her to start shifting so young," she had to admit. "I thought I had more time."

"She is a bit young for shifting, even among my people," Hank told her. "The fact that she's started already means she's going to be a very powerful jaguar, as long as she learns what she needs to know to earn her rank in the Clan."

"And only he can teach her that, Tracy," her father reminded her. "Now that you know for sure she's a cat, you're going to have to make some changes. For Emma's sake."

"I..." Tracy was only just realizing the implications of what had happened. "I'm beginning to see that. I just... I need some time to think about all of this."

"I can give you some of that." Hank's expression was grim. "I'm only here today on a stopover. I'd intended to look you up and see how you were doing. Maybe have lunch together, if you were free. But I'm on an important mission for my Alpha. I have to fly on and fulfill my duty to my Clan." He looked at his watch. "Within the hour, actually. I propose we spend the next little while talking about things, so you have some facts to mull over while I'm away. I'll be back in a few days, maybe a little longer, depending how my mission goes, and we can talk more then. I'm going to try and arrange some time off, and I'm going to spend it here." There was no room for argument in his tone. When Hank made up his mind, apparently, that was it.

Good to know.

Tracy didn't see any alternative but to agree to his plan. It made sense. Even if it scared the bejeezus out of her.

"All right."

CHAPTER 3

Hank flew away from Big Wolf Airport with a pang. He knew, for sure this time, that he was leaving a part of himself behind. He'd felt it before—more than two years ago, when he'd left Tracy the first time—but he hadn't trusted the instinct that said the wolf woman was important to him. Now, he knew differently.

For a jaguar, he'd been very pigheaded, back then. Somehow, he hadn't been able to accept the idea that his true mate might be a wolf, and not at least a big cat of some kind. Even his furry side had been in denial all this time, but the signs had been there.

Why else hadn't he been with another woman in all that time? Sure. Work. Blah. Blah. Blah. It was all just a big excuse, distracting him from the truth. His mate was a werewolf. *Suck it up, Hank.* She was a canine shifter, and he was a feline. There had been stranger combinations, though he wasn't sure when. Everyone knew cats and dogs didn't mix.

Why, then, was his perfect woman a werewolf? The Mother of All had to be laughing Her ass off, watching him struggle with the concept. Hank banked the small jet he was flying onto the new course and felt physically ill at the separation from the woman and child he now knew were his.

The moment he'd seen Tracy, he'd felt like something had slammed into his heart—his very consciousness. He'd missed her. More than someone should miss a mere one-night stand. He'd missed her in his heart. In his soul.

He'd been dealing with that revelation when another had hit him out of left field. The little girl. Emma... His.

She'd shifted, and he'd known immediately. There were no resident jaguars in Big Wolf, Texas. He'd checked. He'd had some kind of misguided idea that, if he knew someone in the area, he could ask them—casually—how Tracy was doing.

Hank kicked himself mentally. That should have been a big red flag. He'd never gone to that kind of trouble to track down an ex-girlfriend. Not even Pamela, and they'd dated on-and-off for years. The fact that he'd even thought to check up on Tracy should've given him a clue that she was more important to him than he realized, or was willing to admit.

He'd been an idiot. And because of his willful blindness, he'd missed out on the first two years of his precious daughter's life. He'd been angry at Tracy, at first, but then, his inner jaguar had stopped him. It couldn't be angry at Tracy over even something as huge as this—not when she'd given him the most perfect little child he'd ever seen. The cat knew he couldn't stay mad at Tracy. Not ever. That's just not the way he was built.

A shifter loved its mate without conditions. Shifters didn't hold grudges with their mates. Neither did they stay angry with their mates. They got the emotions out and dealt with them as a couple, then it was over and they went back to thinking their mate hung the moon and stars, and could do no wrong. The mate was paramount.

And Hank was starting to realize that Tracy was all of that to him. He should've seen it those years ago—and in the empty years since their brief encounter. How could he have been so blind? And how could he ever forgive himself for being that stupid and missing out on the first two years of his daughter's life? If he was going to stay angry at anyone, it was himself.

While he'd never really thought about himself as a father before, he found the role wasn't alarming. His inner cat wanted to play with the kitten and teach it how to be a jaguar. His human side might've taken a little longer to accustom itself to the idea of fatherhood, but once he'd held the little girl in his arms—felt her tiny heartbeat under his hands—he was hooked.

Hank had been looking forward to his mission to Arizona, but now, he just wanted it over with. He had to get back to Texas and work on convincing a certain sexy werewolf lass that she should let him into her life…forever.

*

Tracy watched Hank's plane fly away and felt a tugging in the region of her heart. She'd left work at the restaurant to go to the airport with Hank and see him off. Funny how she hadn't wanted to let him out of her sight until the very last moment.

She'd thought she was over him. She'd thought she'd gotten all those dreams out of her system. Dreams where he asked her to fly away with him on his jet. Where he whisked her away from everything she'd ever known and into the mysterious world of the secretive jaguar Clan.

Not because she had any real interest in jaguars themselves. No, she'd only ever been interested in one particular jaguar. Sexy Hank, the pilot with the mysterious eyes as blue as the sky he roamed and the killer smile.

And now, of course, she had a vested interest in another little jaguar…Emma. Tracy still couldn't quite believe her baby was already shifting. She'd been so cute in her kitten form. Just adorable, if a bit alien to a woman who'd been raised among werewolves…who had pups, not kittens. This was definitely going to take some getting used to.

The rest of the Pack had better figure it out, too. Tracy would brook no harassment of the area's only big cat shifter. She wouldn't let the other kids hassle her daughter for being what she was. Protective mama wolf instincts were clamoring for her to shield her daughter from any possible problems, but her human side knew she had to let her baby grow and survive in the human world, too. And sometimes, humans—and shifters in human form—could be real jackasses.

"Hey, Trace. Hey, Em." A familiar voice called out, finally drawing Tracy away from the window overlooking the runway and the far off speck that was Hank's plane in the sky.

She turned to find her youngest brother, Kevin, walking closer. He was crouching down to show Emma something in his hand, which turned out to be a little rubber super ball he must've had in his pocket. Emma like to chase them around, and Kevin always seemed to have one on him, just for her. He was a good-hearted soul for a stinky little brother.

"Hey, Kev. Doing deliveries?" Tracy returned her brother's greeting. Kevin worked part-time for the restaurant delivering food in the local area during the busy lunch rush.

"Just finished. So, is it true? Our Em is a wildcat?" Kevin looked intrigued by the possibility.

"Who'd you hear it from?" Tracy asked, instead of answering.

"Does it matter?" Kevin gave her a long-suffering, grown-up look, despite the fact he was still very much a teenager. Still, he was growing wiser all the time, which was kind of scary to her. "It's all over the Pack already. She turned into a leopard or something?"

"A jaguar, actually," Tracy corrected her little brother, not realizing until she said it, how proud she was of her clever little girl.

Emma had managed her first shift to and from her beast form with casual aplomb. She made it look easy. The teens attempting their first shift to wolf form didn't always manage it so easily. Every year, a few got stuck in battle form for a while, which could be excruciatingly painful. And some made it to full wolf, but then couldn't make it back to their human shape for a day or two. First shifts were notoriously awkward for werewolves.

Not so for young jaguars, apparently. Maybe it had to do with them being so little when they started shifting. At Emma's age, there wasn't much life experience to interfere with her instincts yet.

"That's pretty cool. I guess her dad is one of them, huh?" Kevin was trying and failing to sound nonchalant, but she didn't mind. She knew anything she told Kevin would be kept in confidence. He wasn't a gossip. He was asking because he cared.

"Yeah. A pilot. He just left." She walked away from the window. Even with her sharp vision, she could no longer see Hank's small private jet. He was well and truly gone. At least for a while.

"Jaguars are really cool. They've got their own secret lair and stuff, according to my friend, Josh," Kevin offered. "And their Alpha is, like, a gazillionaire."

"Mark Pepard." Tracy nodded. Just about every shifter had heard of the man who was trying to lead the resurgence of the jaguar people. "Hank works for him. He's on a mission for his Clan, right now, he said."

"Cool." Kevin fell into step beside her as Tracy picked up Emma and began walking through the small terminal toward the doors that led to the parking lot. "So, when's he coming back? I assume he wants to get to know Em a bit, right?"

"Yeah." Tracy grimaced. "I suppose he has a right to see her, now that he knows about her. He said he'll be back in a few days or maybe a little longer, depending how his mission goes."

"Would you have told him about Em, eventually?" Kevin asked, surprising her with the tough question.

Tracy sighed. "Honestly, I'm not sure. I suppose with Emma shifting now, I would've had to seek his advice sooner or later."

Kevin held the door for his sister and niece as the three of them headed into the parking lot.

"I had no idea they started so early," Kevin commented as

he helped Tracy with the door to her vehicle while she put Emma in the child safety seat.

"Me either," Tracy mumbled, fussing with the straps that would help protect her baby while in the car. Emma smiled at her, playing with the ball Kevin had given her. She rolled it down her little arm and flipped her hand up to catch it, demonstrating her cat-like reflexes.

"Are you afraid the other wolves will go nuts and attack her, being a cat and all?"

Out of the mouths of babes…

Suddenly, fear struck Tracy's heart, followed swiftly by righteous anger.

"I'll bite anyone who so much as looks at her funny." She couldn't help the growl in her voice, and both Em and Kevin looked at her with wary, wide eyes.

She reached down to kiss Emma's little forehead, reassuring her that Mama wasn't upset with her. Kevin was old enough to understand, but when she finished tucking Emma into the car seat, Tracy brought her little brother in for a quick side hug. He hadn't meant to rile her protective instincts, but he was right to wonder.

Wolves had strong instincts about hunting and chasing anything that wasn't wolf. Heck, they even chased each other for fun, when they were in their fur. Tracy would have to be super vigilant with Emma going furry all of a sudden. If the little miss escaped her mother's watchful eye, she could end up in trouble all too easily in the middle of wolf territory.

Not that any Pack member would deliberately hurt her daughter, but some of the younger werewolves hadn't mastered the fine control needed over their beasts' instincts yet. Kevin was part of that young group of wolves, which was why he'd probably thought about what would happen if some of his less-stable friends encountered a jaguar kit in the middle of Pack territory.

"I'll spread the word. Subtly, of course," Kevin assured her with a lopsided grin.

He was growing up to be quite the charmer, and Tracy

fully expected him to be beating the girls off with a stick in a year—or maybe less. He had a good heart, and he wasn't bad to look at either. He was at that lanky stage where he was just coming into his full adult height. Kev was probably one growth spurt away from topping six feet, and he was filling out, too. But not too fast. He was still her little brother, and she wanted to keep that sweet childhood friend for a little while longer.

"Yes, I know. You're the king of subtle." Tracy rolled her eyes as she ruffled Kevin's hair then moved toward the driver's door.

"Do you think Emma's going to change again soon? Can I come over and see when she's a jaguar?" The eagerness in his tone made him sound younger than his years, but she understood the excitement.

"I honestly don't know when she'll shift again, Kev, but you're always welcome. You know that. Tell you what. I'll order a couple of pizzas, and you can come over and watch the game with me tonight." She climbed into the driver's seat and hitched up her seatbelt as she spoke to her little brother.

Tracy had moved out of her father's house soon after Emma was born. She'd needed space and time alone with her baby. Not to mention a nursery she could set up and decorate for her daughter. She'd recovered from the birth at her dad's house, then set about fixing up a much smaller house nearby that the Pack owned and rented out.

Tracy could easily afford the rent out of her salary from the restaurant, and once she had the place decorated to her liking—with a whole lot of help from her father and brothers—she moved herself and Em over. They never lacked for company, especially in the early days of their tenancy. Family members and Pack mates dropped by all the time to check on them when they were just starting out. Wolves were like that. Always in each other's business. But Tracy enjoyed it…most of the time.

Once it was clear Tracy and Emma were doing very well on their own, the checkups lessened. People still dropped by and socialized, but it was less frequent now. Tracy usually enjoyed the alone time with her daughter, when they could play together while Emma was still young enough to enjoy her mother's protective presence. It also gave Tracy plenty of time to think.

Tonight, though, Tracy didn't really want to be alone with her thoughts. Or worse—cornered by her father or some other well-meaning Pack mate. If Kevin was already at her place, he could at least run interference if anyone else dropped by.

"Deal. But if Em shifts before that, you need to text me a pic, okay?"

Tracy just shook her head. Kevin had always had the ability to cheer her up, even on her worst days. Today didn't quite rank up there with the worst days of her life, but it had definitely been a shocking sort of day so far. Hopefully, with Hank's departure, things would settle down a bit, so she could think and make decisions and plans, before he returned.

*

Tracy should've known it was too much to ask for a little peace once her daughter had shown the world—or at least the Pack—what she really hid under all that cuteness. Over the next few days, people started phoning to check how she was doing and dropping by her workplace or home, just to say hello. More than one Pack mate seemed to stare at Em in fascination, and a few rather tactless old biddies tried to question Tracy about Hank, but she was having none of it.

When some of the bigger males offered to hunt down *the cat who'd done her wrong,* Tracy knew she had to put a stop of the rumors, once and for all. She picked her time and showed up at the Pack house for the general assembly they held just before every full moon. Most of the Pack would be there to discuss plans for whatever party they were planning to celebrate the howl, as they called it, when the entire group got together to run together under the light of the full moon.

Her father was running the meeting, and she waited until they'd discussed all the pending business and he opened up the floor to new topics. Tracy walked forward, out of the shadows and into the center of the room, feeling every eye on her as she made them aware of her presence. She held her tongue until she was certain she had everyone's undivided attention, then she spoke in a clear, ringing voice.

"As most of you know, the father of my baby came back earlier this week. He didn't know I'd conceived, and it was my choice to hide the existence of his daughter from him until now." She felt the disapproval radiating from some of the older members of the Pack, but she let it slide. She had more to say, and they all needed to hear it. "I don't want anyone seeking any sort of retaliation on him for my choice. And, while I appreciate all the offers of help, and those of you who've felt the need to check how Em and I are doing, please let me assure you, we're both fine, and right now, we need some time together. Alone." Her Alpha bitch was coming out, and she let the growl come into her voice. "Anybody trespassing into my territory, again, without an express invitation, will face the consequences. My wolf is riled up enough without having to deal with busybodies all the time, okay?"

Now, that was probably a bit harsh, but all the *concern* sent her way over the past few days was really getting to her. Wolves were Pack animals, but right now, Tracy needed time alone with Emma to figure things out. It was clear Emma wasn't comfortable with every last member of the Pack dropping by to stare at her. Maybe it was a cat thing, or maybe it was just a child who was very aware of being under scrutiny. Either way, Tracy didn't think it was good for Em, and she wanted it to stop.

Having said her piece, she backed away before anybody could say anything. Actually, she thought they were all a bit stunned by her declaration, which served them right. Tracy had been a little too docile since she'd discovered she was pregnant. Well. That time was over. The mama wolf was in charge now, and everybody had better just watch out!

CHAPTER 4

Hank was miserable in Arizona. Oh, the people were nice enough, and he'd been welcomed—if not warmly, then at least with little hostility—by the Arizona Jaguar Clan. There weren't that many of them, and they were a closely related, extended family group. Not a good breeding population, if they'd only mated with other jaguars, but this group had bred out a lot. There were more than a few human mates in the Clan, and judging by the power emanating even from the youngest members of the Clan, the jaguar spirit was strong here.

It would be a really good thing if Hank could somehow convince them quickly to ally with the much larger Jaguar Island group under Mark Pepard's leadership, but he would play the long game if he had to. Mark had confided a bit of his plan to Hank. Mark was starting with Pax and Ari—fraternal twin brothers who had retired from the U.S. Navy SEAL teams and then gone into mercenary work. They had good reputations, but their willingness to work with other species of shifters and hire out for money was key. The money they earned went back to their Clan, for the most part. Mark had traced it…with some difficulty, which proved someone in the Clan had mad financial skills. Mark wanted all the highly skilled jaguars he could get to help protect the rest.

From all Mark had been able to discover, he believed the twins cared deeply about their people. If Mark could show those two brothers the life waiting for their small Clan on Jaguar Island, he might be able to get them all to come under the umbrella of his protection. But they were proud people, and cats liked to go their own way, more often than not. It was going to be a hard sell, but Mark had to try, and he'd sent Hank as his messenger or negotiator—whichever role was needed.

So far, he hadn't had much success convincing the brothers to visit the island. He'd already stayed far longer in Arizona than he'd wanted. He had hoped to have this settled in a day or two, and it had already been almost a full week. Hank's heart was still in Texas, but his body was in Arizona…and he *didn't want to be here.*

By the same token, he didn't want to fail in his mission either. So, when Pax and Ari invited him to sample the local nightlife, Hank took them up on the offer. The bar they took him to was typical of any roadhouse Hank had seen in this part of the country. Dusty floor. Battered furniture. Low lighting. Complete with pool tables in the back and a few booths along one wall.

Pax and Ari were greeted like regulars, and they claimed one of the big booths in a corner. Hank was impressed with the way they were treated. Sure, Pax and Ari were both huge guys with a deadly air about them, but the staff, and even some of the patrons, treated them with friendly welcome. That was something Hank hadn't expected. Cats were usually somewhat solitary—for a reason. They weren't known for their social skills, in general, though there were always exceptions. These twin behemoths appeared to be one of those rare exceptions.

They had beers in their hands before they even sat down, and Hank was, once again, impressed by both the speed of service and the genuine welcome they were receiving. He must have shown his surprise in some way because Pax was grinning at him as they sat in the corner where nobody without shifter hearing would have a chance of listening in on their conversation.

"We help out here, sometimes," Ari explained, seeming to take pity on Hank's confusion. "Whenever we're home, we like to hang out here, and the troublemakers figure it out pretty quick and go elsewhere."

"We don't really enjoy bar fights that much, anymore," Pax put in, snagging a bowl of pretzels from a nearby table and putting them in the center of theirs. "Grew out of that a long time ago."

"I bet," Hank agreed, reaching for a pretzel. He looked around the room again and realized the calm was likely deceptive. If the jaguar brothers weren't around, this place was probably a lot more...uncivilized.

"It's a little break for Mack," Ari said, gesturing toward the very large bartender who was restocking the cooler. The human male was wearing a leather vest with a number of colorful patches, and had tattoos up and down both arms. Hank took one look and connected him with the rather bodacious Harley parked just outside.

"Yeah, sort of a vacation," Pax agreed, chuckling. "He likes the place rough, but he claims it's a nice change when we're around for a bit. Lets him regroup, or something."

"Mack was Recon," Ari put in, keeping his voice low.

Hank knew all about the different types of elite military units. He'd been in a couple of different Air Forces around the world, in his time. That was one of the reasons he'd been tapped to make contact with the twins. They'd worked together—sort of—a few times. If being the pilot on some of their covert missions was working *together*, that is.

The first time they'd crossed paths, the three of them had immediately recognized the beast they had in common. It was a bond, of sorts. All three being jaguars, when jaguars were becoming increasingly rare in the world, even in shifter circles. They'd met up again, several times over the years, when work brought them together, but Hank hadn't seen the twins since leaving the service, and that had been more than a few years ago.

"So, what's it like, working for Pepard?" Pax asked, out of the blue, broaching the subject Hank had been sent here to discuss.

"Not bad. He's a good man. A good Alpha. He's taking the jaguar people in a new direction, and I believe in his vision," Hank said, laying it all out there. As far as he was concerned, this mission had already dragged on too long. He took a long pull of his beer.

"I don't know..." Ari said, drawing out the words. "I don't know if our beasts were built for all that togetherness. It gets hard, sometimes, even with our small Clan. That's why we still work for hire."

"I understand that," Hank told them. "Our need for territory of our own and the right to walk alone is something we all struggle with, but Mark knows it, probably better than anyone else. If you guys would just come take a look at what he's built—"

"The island?" Pax cut off Hank's words. This was the first time they'd gotten this far in discussion. He'd been headed off more times by elders and children than he could count when he'd been trying to get to the important stuff. It was as if they were all testing how patient he could be. "Is he seriously inviting us to the island? I thought that was all Top Secret?"

"If you guys had let me talk before, you would've known I'd been sent here specifically to invite you to meet with Mark. On the island. I'm at your disposal to fly you there and back again. No strings." Finally! He'd gotten the message delivered. Now, he'd have to wait to see what they decided.

Both brothers were frowning, apparently thinking hard, so Hank finished his beer and signaled the waitress for another round. In fact, when she came over, he added tequila shots to the order. He was feeling annoyed at being here so long when he really wanted to be back in Texas right now, working on convincing Tracy to let him be part of their daughter's life.

When the waitress had left, Ari spoke. "We didn't expect

this. We thought you'd come to deliver some kind of ultimatum."

Hank shook his head. "Mark's not that kind of Alpha."

"We're beginning to see that," Pax said, nodding. "This is unexpected. All the intel we had on him said he was utterly ruthless."

"To his enemies, sure," Hank agreed, tossing back the tequila. "But he sees all jaguars as family. His protective instincts run a mile wide. He wants to bring us all in, so we have a chance to rebuild our numbers and our strength as a people, so nobody is ever able to kill us off, almost to extinction, ever again." That was almost verbatim from what he'd heard Mark say more than once.

"So, you believe he's not just building a power base so he can lord it over all jaguars, like some kind of king or emperor. I mean, we know some of the other big cats have royalty, but we're not like that. You know we're not," Ari said, watching Hank closely.

"I know. And so does Mark. The power structure he's set up is according to the old ways. He's not creating a dictatorship. Far from it."

"If Mark's Alpha, who's his Beta?" Pax asked sharply.

"Do you know Nick Balam?" Hank countered, glad to see Mark's security was holding.

For all intents and purposes, Mark was the only leader of the jaguar people, but that wasn't really the case. He was the political leader, but Nick—who was ostensibly Mark's head of security—was really the protector of the Clan. They shared power in a tradition that went back many, many generations of jaguars.

"Balam?" Both brothers jerked their heads back in shock, mirror images though they weren't identical twins. Still, they had incredibly similar reactions, which probably made them good as a team in battle, Hank theorized.

"That's an old and revered name among our people," Ari said after a long pause. "But we don't know Nick."

"Heard of him, but never worked with him personally,"

Pax put in.

"He's newly mated, as is Mark. They are a stable team around which to rebuild our people," Hank told the brothers, and he believed it with all his heart.

They talked a bit more about the island and the leadership, but Hank sensed he would get no further with the brothers that night. The shots kept coming, and though it took a lot to get a shifter drunk, Hank was well on his way by the time midnight rolled around. The brothers were probably deliberately trying to get him drunk, as some kind of interrogation technique, but Hank didn't really mind. Everything he'd told them about the island and Mark's offer was one hundred percent truthful, so there were no secrets to spill, even if they did manage to question him under the influence.

The brothers were matching him drink for drink, though. So, they were all pretty much hammered at one point in the evening. That's when Hank let a few incautious words pique the brothers' interest, much to his dismay once he sobered up.

Somehow, the twins had gotten the whole sorry story about Tracy out of him while he was drowning his sorrows. He thought maybe he'd even started whining at one point about the unfairness of it all. And he clearly remembered blaming the brothers and their stubborn refusal to cooperate with Hank's mission for delaying him in getting back to his daughter and the woman who was, more than likely, his mate.

Hank had a hangover for the first time in years the next morning when he woke, and all of it came back to him in a split second. He hung his head and growled low at the depths to which he had sunk in the night. He probably had a bit of apologizing to do this morning, and he wasn't looking forward to it. Not with the way his head was pounding.

Water. He needed a lot of water to fight the dehydration shriveling his brain. And a shower. He could smell the tequila and smoke on his clothes, and it made him want to retch. But his stomach stayed steady. Thank the Goddess for small mercies.

He stumbled his way to the bathroom and took a long shower, only coming out when he felt a little better. It took a while.

Hank wrapped a towel around his waist and opened the connecting door into the larger section of his hotel room to find he had uninvited company. Pax and Ari were sprawled in the two armchairs by the window, looking casual, with duffel bags at their sides.

Shit.

They were either planning to kill him and stuff his body in the bags—in pieces. Or, they were heading out on a mission, and he'd missed his chance to recruit them to the jaguar cause this time. Either prospect wasn't a happy one.

"Going somewhere?" he asked, trying to sound casual as he entered the hotel room and began rifling through his own pilot's case, looking for clean underwear.

"Yeah. With you," Pax answered in a brisk tone. It was his words more than the tone that shocked Hank into looking at the man. He was grinning like the cat inside him had just caught a tasty morsel after a long and pleasant hunt.

"Seriously?" Hank had to be sure they weren't just teasing him. And his head was still pounding a little after the night they'd had. "You want me to fly you to the island?"

"Yeah," Ari answered for them both, placing his feet up on the edge of the bed, as if he hadn't a care in the world. "Eventually."

"First," Pax copied his brother's stretched out pose, "we're going with you to Texas. No sense in letting you take on a whole werewolf Pack by yourself. You need us for backup."

"I do?" Hank didn't know whether to be alarmed, amused or just astounded by their presumption.

Both men were nodding at him. "Yes, boy-o, you definitely need our help," Ari said.

"*Most* definitely." Pax backed him up.

Hank wasn't exactly sure how it all happened but they

were airborne within the hour, heading back to Texas. He also wasn't sure how the wolf Pack was going to feel about the incoming jaguar invasion, but he realized he had little choice in the matter. Cats were arbitrary creatures sometimes, and it seemed the twins had taken an interest in Hank's tale of woe.

Pax stretched out in the back of the plane while Ari surprised Hank by wanting to sit in the co-pilot's seat. What followed was an hour of flying where Hank fell into the role of flight instructor. It turned out that Ari had always had an interest in learning to fly and had, in fact, done a number of training sessions at a local airport in Arizona, but flying lessons were expensive, and most of the twins' money went back to the Clan, to help support the younger and less experienced members of their extended family.

Hank didn't mind showing Ari the attributes of the plane. Teaching other members of the Clan to fly was one of his more enjoyable hobbies. It seemed many jaguars had a fascination with flight, and many of the younger members of the Clan living on Jaguar Island could fly multiple craft—both fixed wing and helicopters.

Of course, Hank was aware that Ari could be setting him up. The cunning cat could be playing a totally different game, and Hank might wake up tomorrow morning to find the twins had stolen the jet out from under him. He hoped not. But, really, it would be better to know, now—before they got closer to the island—if he could trust them or not, so Hank didn't see the harm in using this opportunity as a little test. He was a cat too, and cats liked playing games.

There would be many more tests before these cats—more dangerous predators than even most of their fellow jaguars—would be allowed to join the bigger Clan. Hank knew Mark had weighed the options carefully, calculating that the risk of inviting them into the heart of their new territory could pay off big in the end. If they weren't trustworthy, the isolation of the island and the fact that all the Clan's best hunters had been called back to be there while the brothers toured the island would play in their favor. Or so Mark hoped.

Frankly, having reacquainted himself with these two guys and gotten to know them a bit, Hank wasn't so sure even their best could take them on and win. The twins had one thing to their advantage that most jaguars did not. They hunted as a pair. Always. Had from the day they'd been born. That was different from the usual solitary stalk most jaguars preferred, and it was the twins' edge. It was part of what made them a very lethal team that had a reputation for always getting the job done, no matter how bleak the odds.

Hank just had to hope Mark knew what he was doing. Hank's report, which was as detailed as he could make it, highlighted the twins' unique abilities. He knew Mark, and especially Nick, would take it to heart and make preparations before they arrived at the island. The stopover in Texas was actually a really good thing, giving the Clan more time to prepare their welcome for the twin jaguars.

Hank had told Mark about Tracy and Emma when he'd called in this morning to report his success in getting the brothers to agree to a visit. Mark had graciously told Hank to stay in Texas for a few days, to try to set things right there. He'd also said he would begin the routine background checks for Tracy that would allow her clearance to visit the island. If she passed—which Mark thought a reasonable assumption—then he suggested that Hank try to get her to visit at the same time, if at all possible. Two birds, one stone, he'd said, though he'd amended it to be four birds, or maybe three and a half since Emma was so small.

Mark's sense of humor had gotten decidedly silly since his mating. He seemed to find joy in small things, and Hank was as pleased as the rest of the Clan to see it. Mark had been alone a long time, and a mated Alpha was better for everyone. Plus, Mark's mate was as special as he was. She was an architect who was single-handedly designing the most amazing buildings for the island. She had a real gift, and the entire Clan was benefiting from her artistic vision.

She was nice, too. Open-hearted. Even if she was a bit of a

mage. She was good for Mark, and good for the Clan, and Hank liked her. He almost envied the couple their happiness and had thought wistfully a time or two about finding a mate to settle down with, but had never pursued the thought any further.

Now, of course, everything had changed. He had a child. And a potential mate. But nothing was easy. This was no fairytale meeting and mating, with birds singing and unicorns dancing in the background. No, this was gritty and laced with betrayal.

She should have told him. Dammit. She really should have told him.

"Hey man, you hold that stick any tighter, you're going to break it off, and I think we need that to land." Ari's voice came to him in the close confines of the cockpit. Damn. He'd let his mind wander down dark paths. Again.

"Shit." Hank eased up on the knob he'd been gripping. Crushing, in fact. It was a little deformed, but at least it was still intact. For the most part. He wiped one palm over his face and tried to regroup. "Sorry. Thinking too much, I guess."

"No sweat. Just... We're here for you, man. We'll back you up with your woman and the little one. Every jaguar is precious, from the littlest to the biggest. We'll help you, if you need us."

Help him? Do what? Abduct his child? The thought was abhorrent. He didn't want to *steal* his daughter from Tracy. He wanted... Well, he didn't know *what* he wanted, exactly, except to be part of their lives. Emma's *and* Tracy's. Still, it was nice to know he wouldn't be the only grown cat among the dogs, this time.

Because, this time, the wolves knew all about him, and he'd bet some of them might be howling for blood.

CHAPTER 5

A short while later, they were on the tarmac in Texas, just leaving the jet when the ground crew paid Hank a little visit. A bunch of beefy, single male werewolves were growling in human form as Hank exited, and they quickly had him surrounded.

"You're Emma's father?" the ringleader—a man with more tattoos than Hank had ever seen on a shifter showing through the ripped sleeves of his overalls—stepped right up to challenge Hank.

"I am," he declared proudly. No way was he going to be intimidated by this pack of wild dogs.

"You better do right by them," the man continued, poking Hank in the chest.

Hank looked down at the man's finger with a haughty tilt to his head but didn't budge his stance. He was just in the mood for a fight if these assholes wanted one.

"Seeing as how I only found out about Emma last week, you should give me a chance before jumping to conclusions. Also, what I do with my family is none of your damn business, so fuck off."

Hank made to move past the man, but the guy tried to slug him, and Hank spun into action. Before the others could move, Hank had the ringleader on the pavement, his arm held at an unnatural angle that hurt enough to immobilize the bastard, unless he wanted Hank to break his arm. When Hank looked up, surprised that the rest of the werewolves hadn't already piled on, he realized the twins had come down the steps from the jet and were holding the others at bay by their mere presence.

Hank had known the twins were huge men, but seeing them up against the werewolves re-emphasized just how large and intimidating the jaguar brothers really were. No wonder Mark wanted to recruit them. They were a force of nature, all by themselves.

Hank let his attacker up by slow degrees, getting dirty looks but no further violent action from the wolves all around. Hank stepped back, releasing the ringleader entirely.

"This isn't over," the ringleader warned him. "You cats don't give a damn about your kin, but we wolves stick together. We're Pack. We look out for each other."

"And Emma is my *daughter*," Hank told the man in a cold voice. "You don't know the first thing about what that means to me, so don't presume to understand. Tracy and I will come to an agreement between ourselves, and that doesn't need the input or interference of her Pack. It's *private*."

This time, when Hank walked past the man, he went unmolested. It didn't hurt that he had the two behemoth brothers flanking him. Nobody seemed intent on taking on all three of them at once, for which Hank was grateful. The last thing he wanted to do was put any of Tracy's kin in the hospital. That was no way to try to get on her good side.

"You have some nice moves for a pilot," Pax commented once they were out of earshot of the wolves. "We didn't expect that."

"I may be a pilot, but I was also Special Forces. I trained like the rest of you guys, but then, I specialized. Luckily, I still remember a few things," Hank allowed, trying not to sound too smug that he'd managed to surprise the twins. Why was it everyone thought they had him pegged?

Hank liked surprising people. It was part of his playful

nature and yet another game to him. A fun one where he could be many things to many people, managing to surprise them in good ways all the time. He enjoyed it when he got them good, like just now. His inner cat was a prankster. Always had been.

But then, he decided to come clean a bit. He was here to sell them on the idea of joining the larger jaguar Clan, and this was a subtle opportunity to tell them what it was like to be one of Mark Pepard's top people.

"Plus, we have a pretty nice dojo on the island. Everyone who works in security or diplomacy gets lessons in new fighting styles, if we want. Mark sends out anyone who wants higher levels of training to spots all over the world, then those folks bring back new techniques and teach the rest of us."

Hank looked back to see what the brothers thought of that and caught grudging expressions of respect on both faces. Maybe they would be tempted by the idea of higher education—in the military sense and the civilian. He went on.

"We're building several schools and workshops, as well," Hank told them quietly as they approached the terminal building. "The idea is that anyone who's an expert can teach the rest of us who might want to learn something. And if anyone wants to become an expert in something, Mark will pay for their education in the outside world. We've got masters on the island in everything from baking to building bombs. Gunsmiths, and silver smiths who make jewelry and trinkets. The courses they teach are open to all on the island who have an interest."

Hank stopped his sales pitch as they entered the building. The setup on the island wasn't the business of these wolves—or anybody else around here. Except maybe for Emma...and her mother. Hank had really welcomed Mark's suggestion that he get them both to visit the island, if he could. He wanted Emma, and especially Tracy, to know what the Clan was building there, and that there was always a place for them among the jaguars. A place they both deserved through their bond to him.

Because he was bonded to Tracy—regardless of what she might think. The fact that he hadn't been able to even think of another woman romantically in so long should've clued him in sooner, but he had been both stubborn and blind. Probably idiotic, as well. What kind of a jerk didn't realize he'd found his mate?

He must be some kind of defective shifter in that way. Hank refrained from shaking his head at his own thoughts. He was about to be surrounded by Tracy's Pack again. He couldn't show any sort of weakness, or the wolves would pounce on him—or, at least, they'd try to.

And speaking of pouncing... Hank had no sooner walked into the terminal than he spotted the Alpha wolf heading straight for him.

Shit.

"You know that guy?" Pax muttered from Hank's right.

"Yeah," Hank admitted. "He's the Alpha of this Pack and my daughter's granddad."

"He looks like he wants to kill you, boy-o," Ari put in from Hank's left.

"He probably does, but that doesn't mean I'm going to allow it." Hank had to consciously keep the snarl out of his words. This wasn't going to be pretty.

He didn't let his steps falter at all. No hesitation. No sign of weakness. He was meeting the Alpha head on, in the middle of the airport terminal that the Pack owned. *Great. Just great.*

Hank, with Pax and Ari slightly behind and to either side of him, met the Alpha in the middle of the concourse. Tracy's father didn't need anyone else at his side. The entire terminal was full of his people. All of them would come to his aid if he needed it.

"Alpha," Hank opened negotiations with a courteous nod. This was his baby's grandfather. He would be respectful—as far as he could manage.

"You took your time coming back." The Alpha didn't

bother keeping the snarl from his voice.

Hank realized he was growling too. Great. If Tracy's dad went for Hank's throat, he'd have to defend himself, but he really didn't want to get in a fight with this guy.

"I'm here now, and I plan to discuss our situation fully with Tracy. I have a right to know my own child." Hank remained respectful, but firm. It wouldn't do to show any weakness in this confrontation.

The Alpha was still growling in the back of his throat, his beast getting the better of him in his emotional state. Hank didn't want to antagonize the man, but he had to remain firm.

"My granddaughter is a *cat*, for Goddess' sake!"

The statement burst from Tracy's dad, making Hank shake his head. Hank knew there was always friction between werewolves and any kind of big cat shifter, but the Alpha was talking about his own granddaughter. Hank's child. This would never do.

Hank felt more than saw Pax and Ari crossing their beefy forearms beside him. They apparently didn't like the tone the Alpha wolf had used any more than Hank did, but he didn't want to fight with this man. He had to keep reminding himself of that little fact. A fistfight with her father, in the middle of the terminal, wouldn't do his chances with Tracy any good at all. No matter who won, Hank would lose.

Maybe that's what the Alpha wanted? Hank vowed not to fall into any sneaky wolf traps. They were consummate hunters, but they usually hunted in Packs. Hank was the expert at the solo stalk. He had big prey in his sights—his daughter and potential mate. He wouldn't let a lone wolf, or even an entire wolf Pack, get in his way with that kind of prize in the mix. Not if he could help it.

"Emma is a jaguar, of noble and deadly lineage," Hank reminded the Alpha. They'd talked about this before, but apparently, it hadn't sunk in. Or maybe the man just couldn't get past the fact that his granddaughter was a cat. He'd have to figure that out, and the sooner, the better. "Emma is powerful to be shifting so young. It's a sign from the

Goddess that my child has a strong jaguar spirit. And I intend…" Hank kept talking, not giving the Alpha time to interrupt, "…to teach her the ways of her people."

"*We're* her people," the Alpha growled. "She's blood of my blood. Don't you forget that."

"I will not, but you also have to see that she needs to be around other jaguars on occasion, to learn the things jaguars need to know. Her spirit is that of a lone hunter, not a Pack hunter. She will need to understand what makes her different as she grows and understand there's nothing wrong with being what she is."

The Alpha glowered. "She should've been a wolf."

Hank took an aggressive step forward, and the Alpha met him halfway. Was Tracy's father trying to provoke a fight?

"She is as the Mother of All intended for her to be. We all must accept Her will." Hank tried to calm the situation down a bit. "And, there's Tracy to consider. She must decide how best to raise our daughter, though I hope to convince her to allow me greater input than she has until now." Meaning—any input at all. But Hank thought he had phrased that very diplomatically, if he did say so himself.

"Is that what you've come here to do?" the Alpha asked with a sneer. "Why did you feel the need to bring two goons with you? Were you afraid of the reception you'd get showing your face here now that we all know the truth?" The Alpha was angry, but so was Hank.

"That's Master Chief Goon, to you, buddy," Pax murmured loud enough for them all to hear. In any other situation, Hank would have laughed at the unexpected humor, but things were too serious at the moment to risk it.

"Not that the inner workings of the jaguar Clan are any of your business, but these are the men I was sent to find. They are my mission. A mission set by *my* Alpha," Hank insisted, not backing down an inch. "If you have a problem with their presence, you should take that up with Mark Pepard."

Few men in the world would go head-to-head with one of the richest and most powerful men on the planet. Even among shifters, Mark was in a class of his own, and everybody knew it. He was the reason jaguar shifters were no longer on the brink of extinction. He was the reason they had hope for the future, and most shifters knew it, and respected him for it.

The wolf Alpha shook his head and let out a gusty sigh. Hank sensed the tension of the moment decreasing. Perhaps they wouldn't come to blows right here in the middle of the airport terminal.

This time.

"I've got no beef with Pepard," the Alpha said after a moment's pause. "You two, on the other hand…" The Alpha favored Pax and Ari with a stern look. "You need to behave yourselves when you're here at the courtesy of my Pack. Don't start any fights."

"We don't start them, Alpha," Pax said innocently enough.

"But we do finish them," his twin completed the thought, and the Alpha frowned at them.

Hank held up his hands, palms outward. "They'll be on their best behavior. We all will. We understand the consideration you've shown in allowing us to be here, among your Pack for a short time."

"Just how short is *short?*" the Alpha wanted to know.

"My mission is to bring these two men to my Alpha. I've been given dispensation to stay here a few days in order to speak more with Tracy and get to know Emma a bit." He might have told the wolf Alpha that he hoped to bring the girls back to Jaguar Island for a visit, but there was no way he was telling Tracy's father his plans before asking Tracy, herself. "Alpha, this is Pax Rojas and Ari Rojas, both former Master Chiefs in the U.S. Navy SEAL teams." Hank figured a formal introduction was only the polite thing to do. It also warned the Alpha that the two men weren't just muscle-for-hire, and that they wouldn't take any shit from anybody.

The Alpha offered his hand. "Joe Villalobos," he said to Pax as they shook hands. Then, he turned to Ari.

"We've had all our shots, and we know how to behave in

polite company," Ari put in, shaking the Alpha's hand.

The faintest hint of smile that ghosted over the Alpha wolf's face gave Hank hope.

"And I'm sure you know this, but I'm Heinrich Schleichender. Most people call me Hank." He watched the Alpha's reaction to his full name. He didn't have to wait long.

"Heinrich? What kind of name is that for a jaguar shifter?" The Alpha turned, and they all started walking again. The confrontation had all but ended, but Hank was still wary.

"My father was German. Human. He came to Argentina after World War Two. And yes, he was one of the soldiers on the wrong side of that conflict. Not a really bad guy, or my mother would never have mated him. Jaguars, as you know, are native to the Americas, mostly South America nowadays, and we're somewhat solitary except for family groups. Many jaguars mate with humans or Others, which we believe has made our magic stronger over the generations."

"Well, damn." Joe Villalobos's steps slowed, and he turned to look at Hank. "World War Two? You're probably older than I am. Not by much, but… I wanted someone Tracy's age for her. Someone she could relate to. My mate was of a different generation, and that made it tough for us sometimes. I didn't want my daughter to have to deal with that. And now, her baby being a different species..." The Alpha wolf shook his head. "You two sure aren't making this easy."

"It is as the Goddess wills," Hank said, feeling philosophical. He'd had a lot of time to think about this situation over the past few days. "I didn't expect it. I don't really know how it's all going to work out. But I do believe that your daughter is my true mate. I want a chance to try to convince her of that and make a family with her and Emma. I know it's not going to be easy, considering how we started, but I think Emma should have a father and access to her own species as she grows."

Joe ran one hand through his hair, sighing again. "That's fair, I guess." The words were grudging, but the fact that he made the admission meant a lot. "I can't say I like all this, but I do see your point."

It was a start. At least Tracy's dad was listening to Hank, not just reacting. Now, if Hank could just get Tracy to do the same.

"I will, of course," Hank said, "support my daughter in whatever way she needs, including financially. I've already set wheels in motion to create a trust account for her—for Tracy to use for Emma's needs, in whatever way she thinks best. I have no intention of being a deadbeat dad."

"That's good to hear, though I can provide for my daughter and granddaughter, and have been doing so from the beginning." The Alpha sounded insulted, which hadn't been Hank's intent.

"I thank you for that, Alpha," he said, respect clear in his tone. The last thing he wanted to do was alienate Tracy's family. "Had I known, I would have been here for them both. I'm grateful Tracy had your support and love to see her through what must have been a tough time."

Joe sighed heavily. "My daughter never has done anything the easy way, ever since she was a pup. She should've told you, and I told her that from the moment she revealed she was pregnant. It was wrong to keep Emma a secret. Babies need both their parents. Shifter babies even more so."

Joe sounded a little more sympathetic, which lifted Hank's hopes. He knew he would need allies in the fight to be part of Tracy and Emma's lives. The more, the better.

"Any idea where I could find Tracy?" Hank asked.

He had a bit of time—more than he'd hoped for—but he still didn't want to waste any of it. He had a woman to convince of his plans and a little girl to get to know.

CHAPTER 6

Tracy was enjoying a rare day off from work. She had taken Emma into town to go shopping for new clothes. Emma was growing rapidly now, and she was also shapeshifting, which meant a few of her outfits had been destroyed in the process. Tracy didn't know how jaguar mothers dealt with it, but she'd opted to buy stretchy clothes for her daughter that hopefully wouldn't be completely ruined when Emma changed form.

They were on their way back from their shopping excursion, and Emma had been promised ice cream. There was a Pack-owned coffee shop near the airport that had an old-fashioned counter where soda was still served from a fountain and a soda jerk mixed up floats to order. He also scooped up ice cream with whip cream and sprinkles, and a cherry on top, much to Emma's delight.

They were sitting at the counter, Emma getting more ice cream on her face than in her mouth when Tracy's hackles rose in warning. A familiar scent came to her, and she turned to face the doorway. Sure enough, there he was.

Hank. Hunky Hank, standing in the sunlight, his golden hair gleaming as he took off his aviator sunglasses. She vaguely registered two big men coming in the door behind him then taking up almost guard-like stances on either side, but really, her focus was on Hank. The father of her baby.

The hottest man she'd ever had in her bed.

He spotted her, and his lips rose in a smile. Damn. He looked good enough to eat. He ambled over, his two giant shadows keeping pace behind him.

"Hi, Tracy." His deep voice sent a rumble of desire through her midsection. He held her gaze for a beat longer than was strictly polite then turned his attention to Emma. His smile turned tender and indulgent. "And who's this little ice cream monster? Is that Emma under all that chocolate?"

Emma giggled and went back to demolishing the scoop of chocolate ice cream in her dish. She wasn't very good at using the spoon, but Tracy let her try because little Miss Emma was fiercely independent and wanted to do things by herself. Tracy figured it was better to let her try and figure things out—especially something like this that couldn't hurt her.

Being a shifter child, Tracy knew Emma was ahead of the curve for human babies of the same age. Werewolf cubs were the same. Fast to mature, like their animal counterparts. But jaguar babies were even more...magical, Tracy supposed...shifting so young.

Tracy became aware of the two men who had entered with Hank, who were now smiling at Emma. Protective instincts rose in a flash. Who were these big guys? Had Hank brought them here for some nefarious reason? She hadn't thought he'd stoop to kidnapping, but she'd done a hurtful thing in not telling him about his daughter. Was she really so sure he wouldn't do anything...crazy?

"Tracy, allow me to introduce Pax and Ari Rojas. They're riding with me for a few days," Hank said, looking around, seeming to evaluate every other person in sight.

"It's all right," Tracy told him. "This is a Pack business, and there aren't any humans in here at the moment. They come in on the weekends, mostly, or at lunchtime. During the off-peak hours, it's mostly just us shifters, and we have a system for alerting our people when humans are in the building. See that light above the pharmacy desk in back?" She pointed to the light in the corner of the building, up on the wall, where it was visible from all points in the small building. "When that's lit, we are not alone."

"Good to know," Hank replied, his expression losing a bit of the edge of caution. "Then, I suppose I'm free to say that these men are the reason I was sent to Arizona. I was tasked with picking them up and delivering them to my Alpha for a meeting."

Tracy's heart dropped. "Then, you'll be leaving again?" She hadn't meant to say it, but she seemed to have no control over her wayward mouth.

"Not right away," Hank told her, his voice dropping to a more intimate tone. There was a sort of hopeful expression in his eyes, if she was reading him right. "We're cleared to stay here for a few days, as long as it's okay with you."

"You really should be asking my dad," she said, backpedaling as fast as she could. Did she really want Hank to stick around? Was that the right thing for her? For Emma?

"Already done. He met us at the terminal, actually." Now Hank's expression seemed a little chagrinned.

Oh, no. Her father must've gone to the airport to have it out with Hank. A showdown in the terminal. Great. Just what they needed.

"Was there bloodshed?" Tracy looked at the two giant men behind Hank, searching for signs of a recent fight.

"Nah," Ari said, shrugging his massive shoulders. "Hank handled the baggage boys that tried to jump him on the tarmac."

Tracy felt her eyes widening. He'd been attacked even before he got to the terminal? She checked Hank over for signs of injury, but he looked crisp and clean in his white button-down shirt and jeans.

"Your father was a polite pussycat compared to that mob," Pax put in from Hank's other side. He looked around, finally moving to test the strength of one of the stools attached to the old-fashioned soda counter. He wasn't a fat man. He fit into the space, though his muscles made it a tight fit. He caught the attention of the soda jerk—a teen named

Rusty who had red hair and shifted into a wolf with red-tipped fur—and ordered two large root beer floats as if he hadn't a care in the world.

"Nice to meet you, Miss Tracy," his brother said politely, then nodded and joined Pax at the end of the counter, giving Tracy and Hank the illusion of privacy.

Tracy wanted to ask Hank where he'd found those guys but refrained from any hint of sarcasm. The men were nice, really, if a bit odd.

"They're twins," Hank explained, as if he could read her mind. He shrugged. "You've heard how twins are. They always seem to be on a different plane than the rest of us, somehow."

That was it exactly, she thought. The few sets of twins she knew who were shifters were always a bit odd. Of course, twin shifters were really rare. The fact that the two giants sitting at the end of the counter weren't identical was significant. Identical twins were only born on special occasions when the Mother of All was providing leadership for the next generation—or so it was believed.

Identical twin shifters were protected and guided as they grew because only they could become Lords over all shifters in their region. There were Lords who ruled over North America, another set in South America, and several other sets ruling in other regions around the world, but that was it. The only identical twin shapeshifters of their generation. Goddess touched. Born to rule over all the other species.

The current Lords in her region were werewolves. Rafe and Tim, who were mated to Allie, a human woman of immense magical and spiritual power. A priestess of the Lady. Lords were always mated to a priestess in a rare triple marriage. Tracy didn't know how it all worked, but somehow, it did—and had—for centuries untold.

"Look, Tracy, I was wondering if we could get together someplace quiet and talk," Hank asked, his voice dropping low so as not to be overheard too badly.

There was no help for the fact that everyone in the store

had shifter hearing. They probably heard everything, but at least Hank was trying to signal the desire for privacy. Most wolves would respect that, even if they were still listening. They'd pretend not to, at least while anybody was looking.

Tracy thought through her options. She knew she couldn't avoid this any longer. She did need to have a serious conversation with the father of her baby. Her day of reckoning had finally arrived.

"Yeah. Okay." She ran a hand over her hair, knowing she had to do this, but not looking forward to it. "Um...what if I made dinner? We could eat together, then you and I can talk after. Em usually plays for a bit then goes to bed around eight-thirty. Dinner's at six. Come by a bit before that. Say five-thirty?"

"That sounds good. Can I bring anything?"

She noticed his look at Emma. The longing in his eyes that he tried to hide. He wanted to get to know his daughter.

"If..." Damn. She didn't want to do this, but she owed him a lot more than just an afternoon with his daughter. "If you wanted to come earlier, you could help supervise Emma while I'm cooking. She's been going jaguar every afternoon lately and running around the kitchen while I'm cooking."

Hank chuckled. "I bet that's a barrel of laughs." His sarcasm had an indulgent edge. "Especially when you've got hot pots and pans in your hands."

"Yeah, it's...different. And a little worrisome," she admitted, even though she didn't want to show any sort of weakness Hank might be able to exploit later.

She had her guard up. She had to. Hank's Clan was rich and powerful. If he really wanted custody of Emma and sued her through the human courts, he might be able to use anything against her. She had to be careful.

"What time should I come by?" he asked, seeming more relaxed now.

"Well, she'll take a nap after this, but she'll probably be up again around three. So, maybe three-thirty?"

"I'll be there. Can I bring dessert?" he asked, going back

to his earlier question, in a different form.

"I suppose." She gave in. What could it hurt to let him do this little thing for them? "Aston's Bakery, just next door, makes some really good cookies that Emma loves. She can devour a whole bear claw all by herself."

"Excellent. Thanks for the tip." Hank looked at Emma, and Tracy realized her little girl had been listening avidly to this exchange, not ignoring them while scarfing down her ice cream, as Tracy had thought.

"Sweetie, Mr. Hank is going to have dinner with us tonight. Isn't that nice?" Tracy asked, wondering if Hank would be upset by the form of address she'd chosen.

"Them too?" Emma asked, looking down the counter to the two big shifters who were almost finished with their root beer floats. "Big kitties."

"You can scent the jaguar?" Hank asked Emma directly.

She nodded, sucking on her lower lip. "Not woof," she said, shaking her head in an exaggerated motion. "Like me." She pointed to herself, then moved her hand around to point at Hank. "And you."

"You're right," Hank said, beaming. "You're a smart little girl. I'm like you. A jaguar. And so are Mr. Pax and Mr. Ari. All three of us turn into big cats."

"I see?" Emma got excited by the prospect and was bouncing a little on her seat.

"Not here, sweetie," Tracy put in quickly. "But maybe this afternoon, Mr. Hank can show you what you might look like when you're grown up." She raised her worried gaze to Hank. "Can you do that? I mean, she'll be safe, right?"

Hank looked completely insulted, and Tracy felt bad, but this was her little girl's safety they were talking about. She didn't trust anyone to shift around Emma. Not when she was still so little. Some young wolves didn't have the best control over their beast forms.

"I would never..." Hank said, seeming unable to finish the sentence. He tried again. "I'm a protector, not—"

"I'm sorry," Tracy said quickly, cutting him off. "I'm

just…" She shook her head and gave him a faint smile. "I'm very protective of my baby. I don't let anyone shift around her."

"Even Unca Kevie," Emma put in, nodding sagely.

Tracy knew she was probably going a bit overboard with the no-shifting rule around her daughter. She'd practically ripped Kevin's head off the one time he'd come to the door in his fur. He hadn't ever done *that* again, even though he was one of Emma's favorite people.

"I'm glad you're protective, but Tracy, that same instinct is in me. I would never hurt her. Not in a million years." Hank's voice had dipped low, and his eyes made her want to believe all the promises she'd ever dreamed of seeing in them.

But that was fantasy. This was the real world. And, in the real world, she was a single mom with a newly-informed daddy that Tracy didn't know very well. Was he out to take her baby from her? Or was he the way he presented himself on the surface? Was he truly one of the good guys?

Tracy certainly hoped so.

Hank left Pax and Ari to their own devices after checking them all into the shifter-owned hotel near the airport. They assured him they could look after themselves for dinner and keep out of trouble. Hank doubted it, but he just shook his head. They were big boys. They could take care of themselves. He just hoped whatever happened didn't make the Alpha wolf revoke their welcome. Hank wanted to stay for whatever time he could now that Tracy seemed amenable to at least talking about their situation.

He'd been so afraid that she wouldn't want to see him at all. He still had to talk to her, but he was hopeful that she'd see reason and be willing to let him be part of his daughter's life. He had other ideas too. He kept thinking about how sweet it would be to have Tracy in his life permanently…as his mate.

His inner cat felt at peace with that idea. No, not just at peace. Eager.

It might not have liked being around the other wolves—with a few notable exceptions—but it had come to look forward to being in Tracy's presence, which was a new and very positive development. It liked Kevin too, surprisingly. His inner cat seemed to look at Kevin as a pup to be indulged and protected. It had decided to take Kevin's welfare to heart, which was surprising. It wasn't often jaguars developed such strong protective feelings cross-species.

Could Hank's developing feelings for Tracy be spilling over onto her family? He hadn't felt protective of her dad. Of course, her father was an Alpha in his own right, with his own, very large, very successful, Pack. He didn't need Hank's protection. Kevin, though. He was Tracy's brother. Also son of that powerful Alpha wolf. But he was just a kid.

A kid Hank had always liked when he'd come through this part of the world. He'd seen Kevin grow up from a scrawny pre-teen to the tall, skinny young man he was today. Hank had always liked the kid, but now, even his inner jaguar was feeling protective toward the boy. Strange.

Hank had picked up a big box of cookies, as Tracy had suggested, and presented himself at her door promptly at three-thirty. She lived in a pretty suburban home that backed onto a woodland area shared by the Pack. She had given him the address before they parted. Only Pack lived in this subdivision. It was a gated community, in fact, with guards at each entrance that took their jobs very seriously. Nobody who wasn't supposed to be here would be allowed in, and visitors were tightly controlled.

Tracy's dad had set it up that way so his Pack could roam free within the boundaries of their own home territories. Each family had a house and as much land as they could manage that backed onto a wild area filled with trees and game trails for the wolves to prowl. It was a really nice set up, and as safe as could be arranged on the mainland. Only Jaguar Island was more secure for shifter homesteads.

When the door to the house opened, Tracy's luscious scent hit Hank first. Damn. She smelled really good. He smiled at her as she opened the door wide.

"Hi, Hank," she said, her voice a seductive purr, though he supposed she hadn't meant it that way.

"Hi," he replied, feeling a little off kilter. He hadn't been so inept around a woman since he was Kevin's age. He proffered the box of cookies, and her eyes widened, even as her lips curved upward.

"That's a lot of cookies," she commented, taking the box and moving so he could go in through the doorway. "Thanks."

He entered, and she closed the door behind him, locking it, he noted. There was probably no need to lock doors in a gated shifter neighborhood, but he approved of her caution.

"Come on through. Emma's in the garden." Tracy dropped the box of cookies on the kitchen counter on her way through to the back of the house. She led him to a sunroom that opened onto a garden filled with flowers and herbs.

Frolicking among the flowers, chasing a butterfly on clumsy paws was his daughter, in baby jaguar form. Hank's heart melted. She was so precious. So cute. So utterly adorable.

"She's been doing that pretty much every day since that first shift," Tracy said, coming up beside him.

"That's normal, I think. Cats are very curious, especially when they're small and learning all about the world. This garden is perfect. Enough scents and textures to keep her entertained for hours on end, in an enclosed space," Hank commented.

"Yeah, I started it when she was a baby, and it's gotten larger since then. Wolf pups—even though they don't start shifting until they're teenagers—are happiest in nature, and one of the other women with kids in the Pack suggested starting the garden. She said we'd both enjoy it, and she was right."

Emma heard them talking and bounded over. Hank bent down, and she batted at his hand with her little paws while he chuckled.

"Hi, Emma. Do you want to see what you're going to look like when you're grown?" he asked gently. "I promise the big cat won't hurt you. He loves you." The little cat nodded her head eagerly, backing away as if to give Hank room to shift, but he turned to Tracy first. "Is it okay?"

"Sure," she said.

CHAPTER 7

Tracy had thought about Hank shifting since this morning and realized Emma needed to see the jaguar. She needed to know what she would become and take pride in the size and shape—the full potential of her beast half. That was something Tracy couldn't show her, and it was something Emma needed to know as she grew up, surrounded by wolves.

Tracy, too, had never seen Hank's beast. She'd never really seen any big cat shifter in their fur. Oh, she'd met a few at the restaurant when they flew into town for refueling or a quick stopover, but they'd all stayed in their two-legged form. Tracy had to admit, she was intrigued—more than intrigued—to see what Hank looked like in his fur.

There was something really slinky and kind of sexy about big cats. Even as a werewolf, Tracy had to admit that. From what she'd seen on nature documentaries, most big cats moved with a sinuous grace that wolves couldn't quite match.

"I'll change inside and walk out slowly. That should be the least alarming for her," he said, grinning slightly, calling Tracy's attention back to the matter at hand and away from her dangerous thoughts about the potential sexiness of cats. Hank looked faintly nervous, and Tracy's heart went out to him.

Damn. She really needed to be tougher than this. What kind of werewolf bitch was she? She'd been so strong and adamant that she could raise her daughter on her own, but the moment Hank of the clear blue eyes showed up in her life, again, she turned into a mush. Tracy shook her head at herself while Hank went back into the sunroom.

A moment later, a giant golden and black jaguar slunk out of her house. Holy crap. She'd been right to worry about sexy cats. Her belly wobbled as he began to walk toward her.

He was massive. And incredibly handsome.

Tracy watched him move, almost mesmerized by the way his spots shifted over his muscular frame as he walked slowly out into the garden. Emma held very still, watching him, and Tracy became aware that she was holding her breath. That wouldn't do. She reached down and plucked Emma off the ground, holding her at waist level, which was about the height of Hank's head in his beast form.

"Sweetie, this is a jaguar. This is what you are. What you will become when you get bigger," Tracy said gently to her daughter, who was still in baby jaguar form.

Hank sat on his haunches and let them both look at him for a few moments. Then, he raised his front paw, and Emma reached out with her own tiny paw, meeting him halfway. They touched paws, and the size comparison blew Tracy away. Even if Emma grew to only half the size of her father, she was going to be a force to be reckoned with.

Hank spread his paw, allowing them to see the claws. Emma tried to copy his movements, and her little claws came out of hiding. Tracy had been trying to teach her daughter not to use them unless she meant to do damage, but it had been hit or miss the past week. Maybe Hank would have better luck explaining how cat paws worked to their little girl. Tracy wasn't altogether certain what it felt like for a cat and therefore couldn't explain it well enough for her bright two year old.

Hank lowered his paw and moved his head to sniff around Emma's face. The little girl in cat form returned the gesture.

She even reached out to lick his ear, and Hank reciprocated with a big lick under her chin and then another one down over her head, where Emma's downy fur lay flattened for a few moments before springing back to its habitual fuzzy appearance.

Emma began to wiggle and move her limbs in a clear signal that she wanted to be put down. Tracy complied but kept Emma close, wary even though Hank had made no outwardly hostile moves. It would take time to build trust. Not long, but more than just a minute or two.

Emma scampered away into the herb garden then jumped out in front of Hank, apparently trying to play a furry version of peekaboo, or maybe pounce. Hank was calm as he walked at Tracy's side. She led him to the old oak tree at the back of the yard where she'd put a garden bench in a small clearing. She could watch Emma play from back there, and often did just that. Today, she would share the spot with Hank, she decided, and let Emma come and go at will so she could get used to him.

"We can sit back here and keep an eye on the entire garden," Tracy told Hank as he padded beside her.

He lay down next to the bench, his long tail swishing occasionally from side to side. He was majestic. There was just no other word for him.

Tracy sat, watching Emma approach, cautiously at first. When Hank made no move to stop her, Emma grew bolder, walking up and reaching out with one little paw to touch him, then she patted his side. Eventually, she seemed to find some fascination with the tip of his tail, chasing it from side to side for a bit while Tracy fought not to laugh. Her baby was still very uncoordinated in both forms, but she did try, and she was getting steadier every day. Even in the few days since she'd been shifting, Tracy had already noted a marked improvement in her walking on four feet instead of two.

Hank seemed to watch Emma out of the corner of his eye, indulging his daughter as she began to climb onto his back. Or, at least, tried to. She slipped off more than she climbed, but the little jaguar seemed to think it was fun, so neither Tracy nor Hank objected.

Eventually, Emma tired herself out and curled into a little ball of fur along Hank's flank. He moved a little, curling around her just the tiniest bit, offering her shelter. That was it. Emma went out like a light in a total nap attack.

After a little while, Tracy bent down and picked up her sleeping daughter. She hadn't shifted, but Tracy knew she probably would at some point during her nap and wake in human form. Tracy carried Emma inside and up to her room, placing her on the soft mattress and tucking her in. She then laid out clothes for the child to wear when she resumed her two-legged shape and tiptoed out of the room to get dinner started, and face Hank.

Tracy found Hank in the sunroom, just buttoning the last button on his shirt. Damn. She'd missed the show. Her inner hussy of a wolf wanted to whine, but Tracy clamped down on that instinct.

"You were very patient with her," she said, focusing on Emma instead of her need to see this man naked, once again. It had been far too long a dry spell.

"I like kids," he said. "I've never had one of my own before, but since I'm known as one of the pranksters of the Clan, the others seem to trust me with their little ones when I'm home."

"Home? You mean that island, right? The one Mark Pepard bought?" She'd been curious about the jaguar situation for a long time, and now, of course, she had a special reason to be interested. Emma might, one day, take her place among the Jaguar Clan.

"Yeah. Worst kept secret in the shifter world, but we also have some of the tightest security on the planet. Nobody gets onto the island without our knowledge and permission." He looked hard for a moment, then his expression gentled. "I already talked to Mark about you and Emma. You are both welcome there. Anytime."

Tracy sucked in a breath, completely surprised. She hadn't expected that. Not at all.

"Well, that's... That's great," she said, knowing she sounded lame.

She moved into the kitchen, knowing he would follow her. She needed to start dinner, and bustling around the kitchen would give her something to do besides look into his blue eyes and think about things that could never be.

"You know, I opened an account for Emma last week. I can send you the details if you give me your email address. It's for you both. Something I should've done—would've done—had I known." His voice was soft, as if he was feeling his way with this topic.

Tracy felt the flush creeping up her cheeks. She wasn't a charity case.

"I don't want your money, Hank. I don't need it, but it was good of you to offer."

She heard Hank sigh and didn't dare look at him. Instead, she went to the refrigerator and started gathering things she needed. She didn't want to have this conversation at all but knew they needed to get it out of the way.

"Look, it was my decision to do this on my own. If I'd needed your money, I would've looked you up two years ago."

"But you didn't."

His words fell in the quiet room, and she could hear the accusation in his tone. Too bad. She was protecting her child. If she'd hurt him in the process, so be it.

Her inner wolf was conflicted. Emma was more important—wasn't she? The wolf had always agreed before, but now... Tracy was confused.

"Tracy, money isn't the only thing I have to offer, but I do want you to know that I don't expect you to foot the bill for everything in our daughter's life. I know you're an independent woman, and I admire that, but it's only fair that I pay for some of this." She growled. She couldn't help herself. "Okay. We'll circle back to that another time. The thing is..."

She was so surprised he'd given in so easily, her inner wolf stopped growling and listened attentively for what he might come up with next.

"The thing is," he repeated, his tone softening, "I want to be part of Emma's life. Now that I know she exists, I can't just ignore the fact that I have a daughter."

Tracy knew that. She had known that all along. Perhaps it had been selfishness that had made her keep the secret as long as she had. She loved her little girl and didn't really want to share her, but she knew Hank had a right to know his child, even if Tracy wasn't altogether happy with it. She was very possessive of her baby. She'd had to be, knowing that Emma might grow up to be so very different than her cousins in the Pack. And then, she'd shifted, and Tracy's protective instincts had ratcheted up to an all-new high. But there was one thing she needed to know.

"Why did you never come back?" she asked. "It's been almost three years. Where've you been all this time?" She hated the needy sound of her own voice, but she had to know.

Somewhere, deep inside her, during her pregnancy, and even after, she'd held some kind of misguided hope that he would magically appear and make everything all right. He hadn't, and she'd sucked it up and went on with what had to be done. A few months after Emma was born, Tracy had finally given up on her Prince Charming ever waltzing back into her life.

"I wanted to," he answered in a low voice. "I tried, but it seemed like every time I had a free moment and planned to come back here, some crisis popped up in another part of the world that only I could deal with for the Clan. Since I left here the first time, I've been to Cambodia, Iceland, Iran, Turkey, Peru, and Nova Scotia, just to name a few. Those were the longer missions that took a few months each. In between those, there were always little fires that needed to be put out in Europe, the Middle East, India and South America. I spent a lot of time in Argentina, dealing with my extended family, helping them move to the island." He sighed heavily. "Every time I thought I had some free time coming up, I planned to come here and see you again, and every time, I got a call from Mark or Nick or one of my family members, needing me to help with something only I could help them with. It was like everything was conspiring against my return. Like Fate didn't want me to see you again."

"Until now," she said slowly, really listening to his words.

Had Fate kept them apart for a reason? Was the Goddess playing games with their lives? Was there some kind of higher purpose to all this? She honestly didn't know. What she did glean from his words was that he had been thinking about—even planning—to come back to her all that time.

He hadn't succeeded in getting back here until now, but he'd at least thought about her. It actually sounded like he'd thought about her a lot. Knowing that, she felt a little chink in the wall she'd built around her heart begin to form.

"Until now," he agreed, his tone growing more intimate as he stepped just one step closer, lessening the gap between them both figuratively and literally. "I don't know why it worked out this way, but it feels almost like... I don't know..." He ran one hand through his golden hair. "Like, maybe... For some reason, it was meant to be this way." He sighed heavily, and a look of frustration passed over his handsome face. "Only the Mother of All knows why, but why else was it so hard for me to get back here until now?"

She paused, considering his words, then finally, shook her head. The workings of the Goddess had always been a mystery to her. She had faith in the Mother of All, but she'd never seen the deity she served acting directly in her life before. Was that what had happened here? She just wasn't sure.

"Look, I won't stop you from seeing Emma," Tracy finally said, every word chiseled out of her heart. "Especially now, she needs another jaguar in her life to show her what she needs to know. What I can't teach her."

Admitting that nearly crushed her. She had been

everything to Emma from the day she was born. Now, there was something in Emma's life that Tracy couldn't help her with. A wolf couldn't really show her daughter how to be a jaguar.

"I'd like you both to come to the island. Meet the Clan. Get to know us and see what we're all about. I think it will help you raise our daughter if you understand more about what her animal needs to be happy." He took a breath and continued in a deeper tone. "Come with me when I bring Pax and Ari to their meeting. I can fly you back anytime, but the brothers will probably need a ride back to Arizona anyway, and I can bring you back with them, if you like. It's only for a few days, but I want you to see the place."

The invitation took her breath away. It was one thing to consider going to that faraway island sometime in the future, but Hank was talking about right now. In the next couple of days. Too soon, her wolf howled. Too soon to take her baby away, even just by introducing her to her own kind. Too soon! The wolf woman wanted to weep.

Then again... As she settled her inner wolf once more, she began to think through the possibilities. She'd been intrigued by the idea of Jaguar Island ever since she'd first heard about it. Hank was offering a free ride, which would save a great deal of bother and money, since he had already secured approval to take them. The wolf started thinking strategically. It would be better to know what they were up against...Clan vs. Pack. Jaguars vs. wolves.

"I'm not sure," she told him, trying to sound calmer than she felt. "I'll have to think about it."

"Do that. And, while you're at it, consider this. I'm willing to buy a house or condo near here, if that's what it takes. I want to be here for Emma as she grows up. I want to be in her life. And, Tracy..." His voice dropped down low, compelling. "I want to be in your life, too. Not just because of Emma. I came here last week, looking forward to seeing you again, and that hasn't changed. I'm still very interested in you."

Interested. Huh. Was that all? Somehow, her inner wolf wasn't happy with that wording. No, not at all. She felt like biting him.

Instead, she put the casserole she'd been preparing into the oven and left the room before she said something she'd regret. She heard Emma stirring upstairs anyway. Time to get her dressed and back downstairs to work off some energy before dinner. And to run interference between Tracy and Emma's dad.

Hank realized he'd pushed her too far, too fast when Tracy walked out of the kitchen without a word. He couldn't really interpret her mood, but he thought she was either pissed, thinking it over, or completely repulsed. He'd hoped she might be tempted, but he figured that ship had sailed. He only hoped she didn't hate him.

He found Tracy and Emma in a room filled with toys a few minutes later. He'd heard them come downstairs, and when neither had reappeared in the kitchen, he went hunting for them. Emma was playing with a stuffed wolf toy, and Hank decided right then and there to contact the woman on the island who made stuffed jaguar toys for the children of the Clan. His baby should have one of those very special toys, too.

Tracy was leaning against the doorjamb, just watching their daughter play when he came up behind her, peeking into the room. She didn't turn to look at him, though she had to know he was there. He'd scared her off, possibly, with his talk of the future.

"I'm sorry, Tracy," he said quietly.

Her shoulders stiffened, but after a moment, she turned to look at him. Her expression was closed off, inaccessible. She was on her guard against him, and he didn't like it at all.

Hank tried to be patient and just not let her attitude get to him. She was probably afraid he'd try to snatch their child out from under her or something equally diabolical. He had no such intentions, of course. Emma didn't deserve that, and even though his protective instincts were in overdrive, he knew Tracy had done a good job of protecting their baby so far and she was bonded to Emma in a way he was not.

Emma was intrigued by him, and she seemed to feel a natural affinity for him, but he couldn't be sure, at this point, whether that was because she somehow sensed he was her father or if she just sensed the jaguar was like her. It would break his heart if it was just the cat calling to its own kind. He wanted that bond with his daughter. He wanted her to know she could always come to him and be certain of welcome and protection…and lots and lots of unconditional parental love.

But he'd missed the first two years of her life already. He didn't want to miss any more.

That thought firmly in mind, he let Tracy be his guide in the next few hours. First, playing with toys with Emma in her playroom with Tracy, then sitting down to share a meal with them both. He complimented Tracy's cooking, like any polite guest, but he meant it. Tracy had done wonders with a simple casserole, and he enjoyed the meal more than any other in recent memory.

That was due to the company, even more than the food, of course. Sitting there, at the table with Emma and Tracy gave him pangs of regret for the past, and hope for the future at the same time. He thought how it must be to be mated. Sitting down to eat each day with the woman who was your other half, and any offspring that might result of that union of hearts and souls.

Would he ever know that with Tracy? His inner cat was screeching at him to make it happen. The fickle beast had finally woken up where Tracy was concerned, and even though she was a wolf, the cat wanted her. He wasn't being as snobby as he had been about the difference in their beasts. It was as if Emma's presence had changed everything, turning the cat from interest to full-on obsession.

Hank wasn't sure if that was fair to Tracy, but it was what it was. His cat—and his human side, for that matter—had both been having a hard time with the idea of a cross-species mating. Both sides of his being had felt a strong attraction to Tracy. So strong, he hadn't been with another woman since her. That said something right there that he'd been too stubborn to admit.

After that one night with Tracy, Hank had been ruined for any other woman. If that wasn't the sign of a mate, he didn't know what was. Hank might have been very stupid about all this two—almost three—years ago, but he was aware and thinking clearer now.

The simple truth was, he truly believed that Tracy was his mate. Convincing her, though, was going to take some doing. He's blown his chance at claiming her when they'd first come together, and he knew her pride wouldn't let her accept his claims of love now, without a whole lot of proof.

He didn't know how he was going to accomplish the goal of getting her to agree to be his mate, but he knew he had to try. He might've messed up the past few years of his life by being a blind fool, but he wasn't going to screw up his daughter's life, or the rest of his or Tracy's lives, by continuing to be a jackass. He was going to win her heart. Somehow.

They shared a pleasant dinner, both adults focusing outwardly more on the child than on each other. Hank's thoughts were churning inwardly, though he tried not to show it. He kept things as light as possible on the outside, knowing he'd have time to talk more seriously with Tracy after they put Emma to bed.

Tuckered out from her exciting day, Emma went to bed early that night, even though she tried to stay awake. It was kind of comical the way she kept yawning and catching herself as she nodded off. Finally, Tracy took her upstairs and tucked her in, bringing a baby monitor back down with her so they would hear if Emma stirred.

Hank knew baby jaguars slept more than human babies. All the shifting took more energy out of them than normal human growth patterns. Multiple naps throughout the day was the norm for his tiniest Clan mates, and seeing his own daughter follow suit gave Hank a warm feeling in his heart. She really was the most adorable child he'd ever seen. So independent, yet so loving and attached to her mama.

Hank wished wistfully that Emma might, someday, feel the same love of child for parent, for him.

CHAPTER 8

"She sleeps an awful lot now that she's shifting all the time," Tracy observed, coming into the living room where she'd left Hank sitting on the couch with a cup of coffee.

"That's to be expected. Shifting takes a lot of energy. Some of my Clan mates claim the reason the Mother of All makes the little ones sleep so much when they start to shift is to allow their parents time to recover from chasing after them."

Tracy chuckled as she sat on the couch next to him, reaching for the cup of coffee she'd left on the low table in front of the sofa. She saw a large brown envelope on the coffee table. Hank must've brought it in from his vehicle while Tracy had been occupied. She didn't say anything, figuring he'd get to it in time.

She didn't want anything from him. Not really. She wasn't a clingy female, nor was she greedy. No, her inner wolf was a true bitch—strong and independent. Growling at the merest suggestion that she couldn't provide for herself or her daughter.

"There might be something to that," she replied, sitting back then taking a sip of the dark roasted brew she preferred.

"Before you say anything, that envelope contains the details on the trust account I set up for Emma." He held up both hands, palms outward. "I know you can provide for her. Just think of this as a fall-back position. I will continue adding to it every year. Whether or not you use the money is up to you. If you don't need it now, think of it as a college fund. By the time she gets to that age, she will be able to pay for any school she wants with what I'm putting into the trust for her, even accounting for inflation. A certain amount will always be available if you need it, but a portion of the principal will be invested in high-yield funds, so it will continue to grow. If you want more than the available cash balance, that can be arranged within one business day. All you have to do is call the bank. You're in charge of the entire account until Emma reaches the age of eighteen."

"It's too much," Tracy protested. "I don't need it, and we don't even know if she'll want to pursue her education when she's older. I mean, I hope she will, but I won't force her into anything."

Hank nodded. "Agreed. She makes her own choices. But, if she wants an Ivy League school, or to study abroad, I want her to have that option."

Tracy was silent a long moment. She didn't like the idea of taking his money, but he'd set this up in such a way that she wouldn't have to. The money would just sit in the account, earning interest and growing, unless and until Emma needed it.

"I'll take it with the proviso that it's strictly for Emma's future." She still felt a little odd about accepting his money, but as long as she treated the account as something for Emma, for the future, she felt a little better about the whole thing.

"Okay, but use it if you need it. The trust can be your emergency fund, too," Hank told her, blue eyes hesitant and seeming to plead for her understanding.

She couldn't say no to him when he looked at her like that, so she just nodded and tried to let it go. There were even more important things to discuss here. The money matter— while a big one—was more or less trivial when compared to the custody issue.

Hank had never come out and said he wanted custody of Emma, but Tracy knew he'd be within his rights to demand visitation at the very least. She didn't want to deny either him or her daughter the ability to know each other, but she was also a jealous mama wolf who didn't want to let go of control where her baby was concerned. There had to be some kind of compromise, but she didn't know what Hank was thinking on the subject yet, and it had her worried, frankly.

"Okay," Hank said, taking a breath as if going through a mental checklist. "The next issue is more complicated. I know you've done an excellent job raising Emma alone up to this point, but now that I know about her, I want to be part of her life. Of both your lives. Tracy, I think we could make a go of it...together. If you're willing to try."

What was he saying? Tracy scowled. "You want to try to raise her together?"

"As mates," he confirmed, nodding. He didn't look happy about the idea. Or maybe, that was just her interpretation of his very serious expression.

"You're not my mate." Even as she said it, jumping to her feet in agitation, her wolf howled inside her, angry. But whether the wolf was angry at Hank, or at Tracy herself, even she wasn't quite sure.

"I could be," he countered, standing as well, and stalking around the couch to face her. "I'll do anything to be part of your lives. I'll move here. Buy a condo nearby. Even live in a wolf town where everybody hates me, as long as I can be around you and Emma." He sank to one knee, holding her hand. "I'll marry you, Tracy," he said in a softer tone. "If that's what you want."

Frozen for a moment by the unexpectedness of his proposal, Tracy didn't know what to say. Then, anger flared, and she jerked her hand free and stalked away.

"You're ridiculous!" She wanted to shout, but conscious of her daughter sleeping upstairs, she kept her words to a furious whisper-scream. "I don't want a mate—or a husband—just because we happened to make a baby together. If I ever choose a mate, it'll be because he is my Goddess-destined counterpart. Not some medieval marriage of convenience. That you would even suggest it makes me want to bite you! I want a true mate. Hell, I deserve a true mate."

Hank got up slowly from his kneeling position and walked back around the couch. He stood there, just looking at her, his gaze inscrutable while he seemed to think over her words. Then, finally, he sighed, looking defeated and spoke in a gentle voice.

"What if we *are* true mates?"

Stymied, she didn't respond for a moment.

"What are you talking about?" she finally asked, as calmly as she could, when the silence had dragged on long enough.

"In all the time since we were together, I haven't been with another woman. Not one. I just wasn't interested. I mean, I told myself it was because I was really busy with Clan business—and I was—but there were opportunities. Opportunities I didn't take. Didn't even consider taking." He scrubbed one hand through his hair. "That's just not normal, Trace. Not for a single jaguar male in his prime."

Tracy felt something deep inside. A recognition that she had felt something similar. The wolf inside her had a sense of rightness. Of laughing at the human side that was being stupid, in its estimation.

"I haven't been with anyone either," she admitted. "But I've got Emma, and males don't interest me much anymore."

Hank stepped closer to her. "Males other than me?"

The audaciousness of his question made her breath catch. He wasn't smiling, but there was a devilish twinkle in his eyes that spoke to the passion that had remained dormant in her soul since the last time she'd been with him. Only since seeing him again, had her body reawakened. She had to confess, within the quiet of her own mind, that she'd dreamed of him in the week since she'd last seen him. Hot dreams. Erotic dreams. Dreams that made her blush to remember them.

Funny how she hadn't dreamed of anyone else in all that time since she'd been with him. Not even a faceless lover. Only Hank. Ever Hank.

There might be something to his claim, but she didn't want to give him the satisfaction of knowing she thought he could be right. Not now. Not after he'd botched his proposal so badly. He'd have to prove to her that he didn't want her only because they'd made Emma together. Tracy wanted to be wanted for herself.

"You know I was attracted to you," she told him, keeping her words in the past tense, just to keep him guessing. "The proof of that is sleeping upstairs, right now." She scoffed, but she didn't move away as he edged closer to her.

"Some might say she is also proof that we are destined mates. You know shifters aren't really that fertile to begin with and usually not across species lines unless there's a mating in the mix. It could be that I was just too stupid to realize you were my mate when we were together last." He gave her a disarming grin as he shook his head slightly. He really was a charmer. She'd have to be careful around him if she didn't want to lose every argument and end up doing exactly what he wanted all the time.

"So, you admit to being stupid?" she asked instead, challenging him. Her wolf liked challenging him. It made her feel playful and young…and happy.

"When it comes to you? Definitely," he told her immediately, looking not the least bit bashful. "I've been thinking about you ever since that night, and wanting to get back to you. Duty kept me elsewhere, but I never stopped thinking about you. I realize now, that's because there was a bond forming—if we'll let it—between us."

"You really believe that?" It would be so easy to fall for his words. But what if he was just saying this to get to Emma?

What if any woman would do, and it wasn't Tracy he wanted, but Tracy was just the means to get to his daughter?

That would crush her in time. Kill her tender heart and cripple her wolf. She had to be so careful.

"I really believe it, Tracy," he whispered, drawing even closer. His head dipped, and then, a moment later, his lips were covering hers.

Ah. She remembered this. She remembered the stark passion, the luscious seduction of him. The only man who had ever made her feel this way... Hank.

She reached up and pressed into his kiss, enjoying the feel of him against her. The memory of their night together flashed back into her mind, the solid feel of his muscles against her making her want it again. It had been so long. Too long.

She responded before she thought better of her actions. She pushed him down to the couch and climbed over him. The combustion between them hadn't been her imagination. He touched her, and she became voracious for more, her inner wild woman released...but only for him.

She could feel his smile against his lips as she basically jumped him. He wasn't struggling, which made her inner wolf want to howl in victory. She didn't want to fight with him. She wanted to fuck him. Hard. Fast. And all night long.

The thought sobered her momentarily. She lifted her lips from his, realizing she was straddling his hips. They were both still fully clothed, thank goodness, but the position was compromising, to say the least.

"I don't want to be a convenience," she told him, her emotions raw. "I deserve to be wanted for me, not because it gives you a ready-made family."

His gaze went hard, even as he lifted one hand to cup her cheek. "Don't ever think that, Tracy," he said, his voice soft but filled with the command of his strong personality. "You probably should just get used to the fact that, for a relatively smart guy, I can be very stupid sometimes. Or very stubborn. Or even, both at the same time." A rueful grin graced his mobile lips, charming her just that little bit more. "I certainly was where you were concerned. Did you ever think that maybe the Mother of All gave us Emma as a way to kick my stubborn ass into realizing what was right in front of me for the past couple of years?"

"You really believe that?" She wouldn't make herself any more pathetic by asking exactly what he was talking about. If he had feelings for her, he should be brave enough by now to just come out and tell her. She didn't want to have to beg.

His fingers stroked down over her cheek to the line of her jaw, making her shiver in delight at the soft touch. Her big cat could be gentle when the occasion called for it. She remembered that from their one night together.

"I believe I've held you in my soul since we parted after our one night together. I couldn't forget you, and I couldn't be with anyone else. That, right there, should have clued me in, but as I said—stupid and stubborn, sometimes. Sorry."

He shook his head, and she found it hard to hold out against his charm. But she had to know more. She had to have something to cling to. Some word of care. Of commitment to *her*, not just because of their child. She needed something more definite. She wanted clarity. Bold, honest words.

"I care for you, Tracy. Deeply." Those words were good. She liked those words. "I have thought about you almost constantly over the past couple of years, but I wasn't entirely free to come back. And, of course, I'm an idiot. I didn't recognize the signs for what they were. Somewhere deep inside, my jaguar always expected to mate another cat of some kind, if not necessarily another jaguar. I think my beast side was more surprised than my human half when we finally got back here and realized what had happened. It took my cat a while to figure things out, but he's totally on board now."

"Is that because Emma is a jaguar? What if she'd been a wolf? What if we…mate…and have another child, and what if that child is a wolf? Will your wild side reject that child because it's canine and not feline?" These were the tough questions. The heart of the matter.

She got off him and moved to sit on the other end of the

couch as he sat up on his side. He rested both of his elbows on his knees and ran both hands through his hair, blowing out a hard breath.

"You really think I could be that fickle?" He didn't even look at her as he spoke, and she got the idea that she'd hurt his feelings, which made her feel a twinge of guilt.

"Cats have a bit of a reputation in that regard," she said quietly.

That made him look at her, his face a study in shock. "Maybe in dating, but in mating..." He seemed to grasp for words. "When we mate, we're as loyal as any wolf, bear, eagle or any other kind of shifter you care to name. We roam when we're young, and we tend to sow a lot of wild oats, so to speak, but when we commit, we commit fully. End of story."

Yeah, now, she really did feel guilty. "Okay," she said quietly, trying to think of how to bring the conversation back to where she wanted it. "I honestly don't know that much about jaguars. You guys do tend to be kind of secretive, you know."

Finally, he cracked just the tiniest bit of a smile. "You have a point. We cultivate that air of mystery on purpose, but I won't ever keep secrets from you, Tracy. For one thing, you're the mother of a jaguar. You're going to need to know all our secrets in order to raise our baby. For another, because of your link to Emma and me, you now come under the protection of the entire Clan. You ever need anything, they'll be there for you."

"I have a Pack already—" she began to protest, but he cut her off, gently.

"And a Clan. You have both, now, Tracy."

She didn't try to argue further. She knew her baby would need the jaguars. Tracy wouldn't deny her child the people who shared their beast form with her.

"I do care, Tracy. Not just about Emma, but about you. I haven't been able to look at another woman in all this time. Don't shut me out. I really believe you're it for me. My mate. My *true* mate."

Her heart leapt upward at his words. Did she believe him?

Yeah, turns out, she did—at least about his lack of a sex life these past years. He wouldn't lie to her about being celibate all this time. That's not something a man—especially a virile, powerful, attractive man—would readily admit to in the normal course of events. He just wouldn't have said anything. He wouldn't have made such a big deal over it if it weren't true.

She laid it on the line and told him what was on her mind. "I…" She tried again. "I…don't know how to process all of this, but I'm trying. My wolf is wary, but she's very intrigued by you. As is my human side. Wary, but intrigued."

"And willing to give me a chance?" he asked hopefully, moving closer to her, crossing the width of the couch to bring his lips closer to hers.

She smiled. "I suppose I could be convinced," she murmured, just before his lips closed over hers.

He was the aggressor this time, taking her down to lay on her back on the soft cushions, his hard body over hers. She loved the feel of his possession and didn't protest when he took things further.

They undressed each other—just the parts they needed—by pushing at fabric and undoing buttons and zippers, hooks and eyes, wherever needed, but they didn't waste time. No, she felt like they'd already wasted a little too much time talking when they could've been giving each other the greatest pleasure she'd ever known.

She encouraged him with soft nips and low growls when he licked her breasts and then sucked on her skin. She was conscious of not making too much noise with their daughter asleep upstairs, but since Em had started shifting, she slept hard and never woke up before morning anymore. At first, that had concerned Tracy, but now, she counted it a blessing.

Was that yet another benefit to the jaguar way? She wasn't sure she liked thinking that the jaguar way might be better than the wolf way she'd always known, but it was certainly convenient, right now.

"I want you so much, Tracy," he breathed against her abdomen.

She had a few stretch marks there now, but she wasn't too self-conscious about them. She'd earned each and every one of those, giving life. She sort of liked them. And judging by Hank's response as he ran his lips over them, one by one, he did, too.

"You are so beautiful," he told her in a whisper that made her shiver down to her toes.

She didn't really have the brain power at the moment to respond because Hank was systematically driving her out of her senses, but she kept running her fingers through his hair, stroking him. Petting him as he kept moving downward.

When he sat up and divested her of her pants and panties in one fell swoop, she wanted to howl but held it in. Emma might be a good sleeper nowadays, but howling in her home would certainly wake her.

Hank lifted Tracy's legs, one by one, pausing to kiss her ankles before placing her just the way he wanted her. She felt the wetness coming from her intimate space, readying herself for him, wanting him like no other. Why didn't he just take her already? She'd waited so long…

Hank pushed his pants down, freeing his cock, but he didn't come to her straight away. No, he paused. He had something in his hand, and when she heard the rasp of foil, she knew what it was. A condom.

Shifters seldom had to use such things because they weren't fertile very often across species or with someone who wasn't their mate, but Hank and Tracy had already proven they could make a baby. He was right to be cautious. Thank the Goddess one of them was thinking. Planning ahead.

Hank was taking care of her. She felt a little pang in the region of her heart. He claimed to care, and this was one subtle way of him showing her the truth of that claim.

"Not that I don't want another baby with you, but I think we should plan for the next one, if there is to be a next one, don't you?" Hank's soft words came to her as his smile tilted up one corner of his mouth.

He sheathed himself with careful movements then settled between her thighs, his hard cock just nudging the place where she wanted it most. He braced himself on his hands, holding himself above her and looking deep into her eyes. Then, he paused again.

"This is going to be fast. I'm sorry. It's been a long time, and I find it hard to control myself when I'm around you, Trace." His whispered words were accompanied by a trio of small kisses placed all over her face. "You drive me wild, sweetheart. I want you 'til I can't see straight."

"I want you too, Hank. Please, come into me now," she begged, throwing pride, caution and modesty to the wind. She raised her hips, trying to nudge him deeper into her channel. "Please?"

Rather than answer in words, he simply lowered himself into her, moving slow, sliding home. And that's what it felt like. Home.

Hank couldn't believe he'd denied himself the pleasure of Tracy for so long. Had he been completely blind? Yeah, he realized, he had been.

Well, no more. He was with his mate now, and she was welcoming, warm and so incredibly delicious, he thought he might be drunk with the intoxication of being inside her. He tried to make it last, but it had been way too long. Hank began to move, watching her reactions, moving when he discerned something he thought she liked and repeating the actions just to be sure.

He was learning her body. Learning her responses. Discovering all the little motions that gave her pleasure. He didn't stop until she came, and came again, wreaking havoc on his control, but he managed to hold it together. At least for a while.

When she came for the third time, Hank couldn't take any more. He came with her, feeling like the top of his head had blown off, rocketing him to the stars and back again, on a long, lusty, pleasurable journey of delight. With Tracy. Only ever with Tracy, from now on.

Mate. The cat inside purred, and he knew the truth of it without a shadow of a doubt.

"Are you purring?" she asked him sleepily, her gaze meeting his as he opened his eyes.

"Maybe?" he answered, hedging his bets. Did she find it repulsive?

She laughed softly and reached up to kiss him. "I like it," she whispered against his lips, then took his mouth with deep, thrusting, lazy licks. Mm.

They lay together for a long time, but he had to protect them, and the condom had to come off eventually. Hank got up and held his pants up with one hand while he made his way to the bathroom. She was giggling at his state of undress, which he found charming, but when he came back a few minutes later, she was sitting on the edge of the sofa, re-dressed and thinking hard.

He stopped short. This didn't look good.

He'd thought they'd crossed a bridge here tonight, but maybe not. Maybe she'd just thrown him back a few steps. He stifled a sigh. Tracy didn't do things easy. Hank shouldn't have expected his stubborn mate to give in all at once, so easily. He'd have to work at this, but he was up to the challenge. He'd win her, come hell or high water. And he'd cross that metaphorical bridge someday soon, then destroy it, so it could never separate them again.

CHAPTER 9

"You can't be here when Emma wakes up," Tracy told him, finality in her tone. She scrupulously tamped down on the regret. That wouldn't help in this situation.

Hank didn't look happy about her decision, but he nodded tightly after searching her gaze for a long moment. "Okay. I'll go. But think about what happened here, between us. Has anything ever felt so right before?" He moved close, and she held her ground, but all he did was press a gentle kiss to her forehead before letting her go.

He was right. Being with him had always felt *right*. But it had also gone terribly *wrong* in the past. Not that her baby was wrong, but the whole crazy path her life had taken since meeting Hank hadn't been the easiest road she'd ever taken. Known as a woman who liked to do things the hard way, she'd lived up to that dubious reputation since the morning handsome Hank had flown off into the sunrise, leaving Tracy pregnant and alone.

He'd hurt her. Not intentionally. He'd had no way of knowing he'd left her behind with a baby on the way. And she'd been too stubborn to tell him. But the fact that he'd managed to stay away for well over two years... That hurt.

If he'd been thinking about her all that time, why hadn't he come for her? Why wait until now? Why had he made her wait so long?

Did he really want her at all? Or was it just his conscience rearing its head now that he knew he had responsibilities in the form of one adorable little jaguar kit? And what if Emma had turned out to be a wolf? Would he be so eager to take them on then?

She had no way of knowing. She didn't know him well enough to trust him, either. Oh, about certain things, yes. He was a good man, at heart, and he was loyal to his Clan. She trusted in that sort of thing. But to trust him with her heart? Her future? Her *daughter*?

She just wasn't so sure.

Hank left, feeling both exhilarated by what had happened and flat-assed rejected. He'd had her in his arms once more, and all had been right with his world...and then, she'd slipped through his fingers, slipping away from the commitment he wanted so badly. Damn. When had that happened? When had he gone from wanting to commit to Tracy for Emma's sake to wanting Tracy beyond all coherent comprehension?

He couldn't pinpoint the moment, but it had definitely happened. Maybe when he saw her pretty brown eyes peering up at him over Emma's dark blonde curls. Maybe it had been at the soda fountain when she'd gone all protective at seeing Pax and Ari with him. Or maybe it was when they'd sat in Tracy's garden with the sun shining down on her wavy chestnut hair.

He wasn't sure exactly how it had happened or when, but his inner cat was on board with his human half—finally. Both sides of him needed Tracy. There was no other woman who even came close to being what he wanted and needed in his life. Only Tracy. Forever.

But how in the world was he going to convince her of that? They hadn't gotten off to the greatest start. There would always be doubts about his motivations now that Emma was on the scene. But he couldn't bring himself to regret Emma's existence. He would be hollow without her giggling laugh. Empty without her tiny growls. Now that he'd seen her, he would always need her in his life. Always.

Just like her mother.

He needed to mount a campaign to win Tracy's heart. He didn't know how he was going to do it, but he had to figure it out. He had no other choice.

That thought firmly in mind, Hank went back to the hotel where he and the jaguar twins had been given a giant suite that had two separate bedrooms—one with a king-sized bed that Hank had claimed and one that had two double beds that worked for the twins. There was a sitting area with some big chairs, a couch, and a huge television, too. When Hank entered the suite, he was confronted immediately by the coppery scent of blood.

Senses going to full alert in the blink of an eye, he took in the situation. The twins were sitting in front of the TV. One was sprawled on the couch, flipping channels between two different basketball games, the other was in an armchair, doing something to his arm. It was his arm that was bleeding, and the innards of a first aid kit were strewn on the low coffee table in front of him.

A sharp acrylic scent reached Hank's sensitive nose, making him jerk his head to the side. "What the hell is going on here?" he demanded. The twins didn't even look up. They'd had to have heard him walking down the hall long before he'd entered the room, but they didn't seem in the least concerned.

"Numbnuts zigged when he should have zagged," Ari said of his twin as he flipped back to the other basketball game with seeming indifference.

"Fucker had a knife," Ari grumbled, still working on his arm. "What kind of shifter uses a knife in a shifter fight? Fucking wolves."

"You were fighting with the wolves?" Hank asked, moving closer, having locked the door behind himself before stepping farther into the room.

"No choice, really," Pax said philosophically as he straightened from his reclining position on the couch and tossed the remote control onto the coffee table. "We got jumped, so we fought back, trying to do as little damage as possible while still letting those jackasses know we could wipe the floor with them all."

"But one of them got in a lucky shot with a switchblade. Little punk," Ari growled.

"How old were these wolves?" Hank began to get suspicious.

"Juveniles," Pax answered immediately. "Ranging in age from about seventeen to twenty. Immature and full of themselves. Good pack fighters, though. There were a lot of them."

Pax got up and retrieved three beers from the small fridge the brothers must've stocked earlier. He threw one to Hank and put another down on the coffee table in front of Ari, then reclaimed his seat and popped the tab on his own. Hank nodded his thanks before opening his own can of beer and taking a long pull.

"We didn't hurt any of them too bad," Ari claimed as Hank took the chair opposite his, getting a closer look at what Ari was doing. He had a tube of super glue and was gluing a gash on his arm back together somewhat awkwardly.

"Super glue?" Hank asked, nodding toward Ari's arm. "Does that really work?"

Hank had seen something like it in the military, but that had been stuff made specifically for bonding human skin. He'd never thought to try hardware-store super glue for the same purpose.

"All I need is something to hold the skin together for a little while, until the healing kicks in," Ari said absently as he continued to work on the long gash. "That way, it won't scar too much."

Jaguars, like all shifters, had accelerated healing abilities. That was just part of who they were. As a result, they seldom needed things like bandages or sutures. Though, if a cut was deep enough, a stitch or two would help hold things together until a shifter's natural healing abilities revved up and healed it from the inside out.

"It's actually better than using a needle on myself," Ari said a moment later. "This just stinks a bit until it's dry, and somehow, as my body heals, it expels the glue. Looks gross, but this shit works."

Hank shook his head. "Good to know."

Hank decided to pass along the information to the Clan's healer. Jaguars did get banged up a lot, and having sharp claws meant the occasional slice, so having an alternative to sewing wounds closed with something readily available in any dollar store would be good information to pass around the Clan. He decided to put a tube of super glue into his own first aid kit next time he had a chance—as long as the Clan's healer gave the all clear. While he liked and respected the twins, he preferred to have a trained medical opinion on whether or not the chemicals in the store-bought super glue would be safe for regular use.

Hank drank his beer and pretended to watch the game until Ari finished with his glue. The scent of the acrylic was strong, but the air circulation system in the room was sufficient to whisk away the smell in short order. Ari must have cranked the system up before he started working on his arm.

"What can you tell me about the kids who attacked you?" Hank asked finally, as he finished his beer and set the can on the table.

"Not much," Pax said. "Kids. Looking for trouble. Raging hormones. You know the type."

Hank nodded. "Any injuries to them I should know about?"

"Nah," Ari said, sitting back in the chair and discarding the paper towels he'd used to sop up the blood. "We bloodied their noses but made sure not to break anything. They were just kids, after all. Once they realized what they were up against, they tucked their tails and ran home to mama."

"What about the one that cut you?" Hank asked of Ari.

"This?" Ari looked scornfully at his arm. "I've had worse. Actually, when they scented the blood, everybody froze, and a split second later, they started running away. I don't think they'd intended to go that far, and even the blood scent didn't stir their wolves, as I thought it would." Ari looked philosophical.

"These kids haven't been blooded. Not like us," Pax put in. "They were raised here, in their quaint little town. Protected. Safe in their Pack. First scent of blood, they probably feared the censure of their Alpha for an unsanctioned attack more than their wolves wanted the blood."

"Strange way to raise kids," Ari put in, looking at his twin.

"They've been safe their entire lives," Pax said, nodding slowly.

"We sure as hell weren't raised that way. We were tougher at their age," Ari said with a grim tone to his voice.

Hank understood. In the last hundred years or so, no jaguar child was raised in the kind of comfort and safety the wolves had here. Only in recent times, since Mark had stepped up and created the community on Jaguar Island, had there been any hope for the young to grow up in safety and peace, without fear. Without learning what it meant to fight and kill at too young an age.

"I'd almost envy these wolves," Pax said quietly. "But their kids are weak compared to the way we were at that age."

"Be glad of that," Hank told them. "Otherwise, you would've had a worse fight on your hands tonight, and we'd be coming under fire from the Alpha for hurting children."

Ari looked sharply at Hank. "There is that," he admitted after a moment.

"I wonder what it would have been like," Pax mused quietly. "To have grown up so innocent?"

All three men were quiet a moment while they considered that statement. Then, Hank spoke up.

"That's one of the things Mark is fighting for. A peaceful place, where our young can grow up without fear. Free to be just children, not warriors at a young age."

"But then, they'd be too soft. Too unprepared for what's coming," Ari protested quietly, a wistful look on his face.

"Not necessarily," Hank countered. "They all train and are taught. They know that the world outside our island holds danger for our kind. They are never let out into the world unprepared. But while they live on the island, they are safe. Free in a way we never were."

The twins seemed to think about that for a while. It was Pax who spoke, after a long pause.

"That sounds like…" He cleared his throat. "It sounds idyllic."

"It is," Hank told him. "But you'll see it for yourself. You can make your own judgments."

"If we ever get your mate situation straightened out," Ari commented, somewhat sarcastically. "Any progress on that front?"

Hank bristled. He didn't really want or need interference from these two relative strangers, but it looked like he was stuck with them for the remainder of this mission. He couldn't tell them to buzz off. Not like he wanted to. And the smug bastards knew it.

"She sent me home," Hank admitted. "But I think we made great strides forward before that happened."

"I'll translate," Ari offered with a grin. "Our boy got laid." He tapped his nose and winked. Hank knew they could smell the subtle hint of Tracy on him.

Hank growled at the bloody twin. "None of your business," he said, knowing it sounded juvenile, but powerless to keep the words from coming out of his mouth.

Ari only laughed. His twin was grinning too. Idiots.

"What you need, boy-o, is a strategy," Ari said when he finally stopped guffawing. Hank's inner cat stilled. It liked strategy games. And, Hank had been thinking that he needed to come up with a plan, he'd just drawn a blank so far.

"You know," Pax put in from his seat on the couch, "I think her father might help. He seemed very interested in holding you accountable, but he also looked like a man who wanted to see his daughter happy."

"You gonna make her happy?" Ari asked slyly.

"Of course," Hank replied without demur. His number one goal in life now, was to make his mate and child happy and keep them both safe.

"Then her dad ought to help," Pax concluded. "From everything we've seen, he's a good Alpha, with tight control over his Pack."

"You should call him tomorrow morning," Ari said, nodding to himself as if the matter was already settled.

Hank wouldn't be so easily led, but he had to acknowledge—at least to himself—that the twins might have something there. He stood and headed for his bedroom.

"I'll think about it," was all he said before opening his door.

He heard derisive chuckles behind him as he went in and closed the door to his bedroom behind himself. Let them laugh. If it turned out for the best, he'd thank them in the end for their advice. If it didn't, he'd hold it against them for the rest of their lives.

The next morning, the twins were already gone when Hank woke up at seven a.m. He didn't worry too much about it. They could take care of themselves, and they'd shown discretion last night by not wiping the floor with the juvenile wolves who'd attacked them. The more he was around the two jaguars, the more he respected them.

Not only were they skilled operators—something Hank had known from working with them previously in the military—but they were thinking men who didn't abuse their power. He'd seen them at home with their small Clan in Arizona, and they were tolerant of the children and affectionate toward their family members. They weren't *just* soldiers, in his mind, anymore. They were complex beings he felt he could be friends with, if the situation allowed it.

It all sort of depended on what happened when they got to the island. If they rejected Mark's offer politely, then the possibility of friendship was still open. If, however, there was some kind of blow up, then Hank's loyalty had to be with Mark and the larger Clan. The best case scenario, of course, was if the twins decided to entertain Mark's offer and begin the process of affiliating the Arizona Clan to the larger Jaguar Clan. If they could be brought in under Mark's overall leadership, then not only could the friendship develop further—if that's what was going to happen—but they would be allies and Clan mates.

Hank hoped for that outcome. Not only because he found himself liking the twins more and more, but because he'd liked the Arizona Clan. They might be small, but they were as warm and steadfast as any jaguar Clan that had survived this long. They were good people, struggling in a world that wasn't entirely welcoming to their species. Hank knew all about that struggle and hoped the Arizona Clan would join the larger Clan. They'd be stronger for it and would have all of the resources Mark had built at their disposal. They'd be safer.

Hank wanted that for them. And he wanted to add the skills of Pax and Ari Rojas to the bigger Clan's skill set. Those twin Master Chiefs would make strong allies and even better friends. Hank hoped that was the future in store for them all, but only the Goddess knew for sure.

After a quick shower, Hank put on his last clean shirt. He'd have to either do laundry or go shopping if he wanted to continue making a good impression. Dirty shirts weren't going to cut it on this particular mission. He'd have to look into his clothing crisis later, though. First, there was an Alpha to get on board with his plan.

Hank called Tracy's dad on his cell, hoping the Alpha werewolf was in a good mood. Joe Villalobos answered with a snarl in his voice, so no, the man wasn't pleased to hear from him, but Hank forged ahead anyway, asking for a face-to-face meeting. Hank had decided while he was in the shower that this sort of thing had to be done in person. He was basically laying siege to the man's daughter and wanted to convince him to help. That wasn't the sort of thing you could ask for over the phone.

Joe surprised Hank by inviting him to join him for breakfast. Joe named the diner in town and said he'd be there in fifteen minutes. The place was within easy walking distance, so Hank left the hotel room and headed for the diner, taking his time so as to arrive only a little before the werewolf Alpha.

Hank didn't want to keep Joe waiting. It was a sign of respect and just good manners. Hank had to be ultra careful with Joe during this period, because it was within the Alpha's rights to ask him to leave town. To fly away and never come back. Hank would just about die if that happened, and Joe knew it. Therefore, Hank didn't want to give the man any excuse to ban him from Big Wolf, Texas, now or in the future.

When Joe drove up in a battered pickup truck, Hank met him with a respectful nod of greeting. Joe climbed out of the truck and faced Hank, hands on hips, challenging.

"If this is about the run-in the gigantic twins had last night with a group of silly pups—"

Hank shook his head, holding up one hand, palm outward while he grinned. "I heard about that, Alpha. No hard feelings. As long as the pups are okay."

Joe Villalobos just shook his head. "They're fine. Stupid kids." He muttered a few other things that Hank chose not to hear, regarding the idiocy of youth, then led the way toward the door of the diner. "I'm glad your two behemoths held back. Somehow, those boys got the idea I would be glad if they attacked two guests in our town. It wasn't sanctioned."

"We all figured as much," Hank replied quietly as he held the door open for the Alpha.

Joe grunted and nodded, acknowledging Hank's words. He took a seat in a far booth where they'd have a good view of the doorway before he spoke again. Hank sat opposite him.

"So, what's this all about? Why did you want to see me?" Joe asked.

Moment of truth time. Hank took a deep breath.

"It's like this, Alpha. I'm in love with your daughter." Damn. He'd actually said it out loud. "I have been for the past couple of years, but I was too stupid, stubborn...you-name-it...to allow myself to recognize it. I couldn't quite accept that my mate wasn't a cat of some kind, so I guess I buried my head in the sand and refused to acknowledge the truth when it was staring me right in the face."

Joe just looked at him for a moment, then nodded. "You had a case of the stupids? There's a lot of that going around lately. Starting with those kids last night and ending right here at this table. What exactly do you think I can do about your little problem? Which, by the way, isn't so little. My daughter is stubborn as hell, and she isn't going to easily accept that you only just figured this out." He leaned in, staring Hank down. "You hurt her, son. Her feelings are bruised. And I have to warn you—she's not going to trust you easily again."

Hank didn't look away from the Alpha's gaze, which was meant to intimidate a lesser shifter. But Hank had a little secret. He was an Alpha male too. If the Jaguar Clan was stronger and his people more numerous, he'd probably have a Clan of his own to rule over, but the history of the jaguar people had created an odd situation where they all had to pull together under an Alpha-Beta hierarchy just to help their species survive into another generation.

"With all due respect, sir, she hurt me as well. She should've called when she found out she was expecting." Hank was careful to keep his tone cool. Objective. Matter-of-fact. He saw the moment the werewolf Alpha realized Hank had a point. The man eased back in his chair and looked at Hank for a long moment before replying.

Joe shook his head. "Yeah, I told her that. More than once." The waitress came over then, and took their orders.

Hank waited until she was gone before speaking again.

"I missed seeing my child as a baby. I missed her first steps. Her first words. I can never get any of that back, but I can make sure I don't miss anything in her future," Hank said, keeping his tone reasonable. "I can see I need to prove myself to Tracy first. I've seen how closed off she is emotionally. How protective she is of our child. I get it, and I respect it, as far as it goes, but I need to break through. Somehow."

Joe sighed. "You've certainly got your work cut out for you."

"Which is why I'm here. I'd like to get your permission to court your daughter. I know it's all ass-backwards, but I figured I should start over at the beginning." Hank gave Joe what he hoped was a disarming smile, but he could see Tracy's father wasn't completely fooled by the attempt at charm.

"Flowers and candy aren't going to cut it with a strong female like Tracy," her father warned Hank.

"I didn't expect they would," Hank agreed. "If you have any advice, I'd be happy to hear it."

CHAPTER 10

"You're serious about her being your mate?" Joe wanted to know. "That's not just a convenient label to put on the mother of your child?"

Hank shook his head. "Emma is great, but I came back here originally—before I even knew about Emma—because I could never get Tracy out of my mind."

"Took you long enough," Joe grumbled, his wolf growling a bit through his words.

"It did, and for that, I will probably never forgive myself. My only excuse is that I was doing what I thought was right for her, for myself, and for my Clan. I really have been on constant duty for the last two-plus years. My Clan has been in need of my skills, and I wasn't going to say no when duty called. But, always in the back of my mind, was this place...and Tracy."

"How many women have you slept with since leaving her?" Joe asked bluntly.

Hank squirmed. It was one thing to admit this to Tracy, in private. It was quite another to discuss his lack of a love life in the harsh light of day, in the middle of a diner full of nosey werewolves who could probably hear most, if not all, of their conversation.

But...this was for Tracy. Pride had to take a backseat to

the need to claim his mate. Hank might feel—and look—like a fool, but at least he'd be an honest fool. And, maybe, everybody would figure out just why he was so grumpy.

Hank took a deep breath then stated the flat truth as quietly as he could manage. "Not a one. And yes, I know that should've been my first clue that I'd left my mate behind here in Texas, but like I said…stupid. It took coming back here and seeing her again, to realize how completely idiotic I've been."

Joe's gaze measured him. A lesser man would have flinched or squirmed under the intensity of the Alpha's stare, but Hank sat calmly. It wasn't exactly comfortable, but he wouldn't be cowed by simple dominance games like a stare-down. At length, the Alpha wolf spoke.

"Not a one, eh?" A smile broke over Joe's face as he shook his head slightly. He looked impressed, if Hank was any judge of the other man's expression.

Thankfully, the food arrived at that moment, and the conversation halted while plates were sorted out and utensils readied. Joe began to eat, and Hank followed suit.

"In theory, I know that cross-species matings do happen from time to time," Joe said quietly, after a few minutes spent eating steadily. His tone was reflective. "Can't say we've had much of that here, though, so it's bound to take some getting used to."

"That was part of my problem, too. All my life, I thought…if I was ever lucky enough to find a true mate…she'd be a jaguar. Or, at least, some sort of big cat. I never even considered…"

Joe put down his coffee cup and looked at Hank, as if assessing his value, then looked down and shook his head just once, before speaking again. "I'm not sure what to think about all this, but if my daughter is your mate—and little Emma seems to be the proof of that—then…I won't stand in your way." Joe sighed deeply before continuing. "I'll be honest and say my inner wolf isn't crazy about the idea of a cat for a son-in-law, but if the Mother of All has other ideas, then who am I to say nay?"

Hank didn't quite breathe a sigh of relief, but he definitely felt some of his tension ease. With the Alpha of the Pack on his side—or at least, not against him—he would have one less thing to worry about.

"Thank you, Alpha," Hank replied, with all due respect. Tracy's dad was the man in charge around here. Maybe he didn't have quite as much money or international clout as Mark Pepard, but he was still a force to be reckoned with in his own territory. Hank would not forget that.

Hank decided to be as honest as he could be with Joe, since the Alpha seemed to have thought through this situation. Hank told Joe about Mark's invitation for Tracy and Emma to travel with Hank to Jaguar Island.

"Tracy and Emma are still members of this Pack," Joe stated, seeming concerned.

"I'm glad to hear you say that, even considering that Emma carries a jaguar spirit," Hank said patiently, trying to explain as best he could to this man who held such power in this area. "Tracy and Emma both have a right to know more about my people. Mark doesn't let just anyone onto our island, but Emma and Tracy will always have clearance to go there. They are part of the Jaguar Clan, now, too. Whether they choose to use that connection is strictly up to them, but it remains. Emma is welcome on the merits of the animal spirit she carries, and Tracy is welcome based on her connection to Emma...and me."

"I see." Joe looked pensive and a little less angry than he had when Hank had first mentioned the idea of taking the girls away to visit the island.

"I hope to convince Tracy to make a quick trip. Just a visit, really. I just want her to see the place and let my Alpha meet Emma and recognize her formally. I want to build those connections, so Tracy knows she can always rely on them." He didn't say it, but Hank knew Joe was smart enough to realize Hank wanted to make sure Tracy and Emma would know who to go to in the Jaguar Clan in case something should ever happen to Hank.

Life was uncertain. Shifters knew that hard lesson better than most. Although Hank didn't plan on dying anytime soon, his fate—as always—was in the hands of the Mother of All. If something happened, Hank wanted to be sure Tracy knew she had alternatives to the Pack of her youth. He wanted to be certain Emma would have the chance to be a jaguar. To learn from other jaguars and grow up with jaguar friends. That was something that was only available on Jaguar Island, now that Mark was gathering all the jaguars together.

Joe sat back and gave Hank a measuring look. "I can see where that's important to Emma's future, in particular, and I like that you're thinking of my daughter's and granddaughter's safety. They are, and always will be, part of Big Wolf Pack, but even I can see the advantages of affiliation with an Alpha of Pepard's stature." Joe seemed to relax a fraction. "I'll support your efforts to get her to visit, but I'm not prepared to have either Tracy or Emma stay on that island permanently. I want your assurance that, if they go, they have the freedom to leave any time they want."

"You have my promise, of course," Hank was quick to reply. "I would never keep either of them against their will. I'll fly them out myself anytime Tracy wants. It's all up to her. But I'll go one further for you. I'll have Mark give you a call—Alpha to Alpha—so you can be reassured of their safety and freedom to come and go."

"You're on a first name basis with Pepard? He'll do that kind of favor for you?" Joe asked, seeming a bit skeptical.

Hank nodded slowly. "Mark and I go way back. I'm a troubleshooter for the Clan, and I have the Alpha's confidence, his permission to negotiate on behalf of the Clan in certain matters, and his friendship. I'll set up the call."

Joe seemed to think about that for a moment, then nodded. "Have him call me before you leave, if Tracy agrees to go with you. Otherwise, I'm prepared to trust your word...for now."

They spent the next few minutes discussing strategy, and

Joe proved to be a good accomplice.

Tracy wasn't sure why she invited Hank to dinner again, later that day. He came into the restaurant for lunch, and she immediately sensed his presence. When she walked into the dining area from the back, she noted the hushed way her Pack mates were watching the lone cat in the room as he ordered his food and handed the menu back to the teenager who was waitressing in his section.

Young Millie seemed flustered and barely squeaked when she spoke to the jaguar. Tracy chuckled as the girl went on her way with Hank's order, and Tracy decided, right there, to take the bull by the horns. She very deliberately walked calmly over to his table and sat down opposite him, daring her Pack mates to take exception. None did.

She wasn't the daughter of an Alpha for nothing. Since becoming a mom, Tracy had found her own deeply rooted power. She'd become aware of her place in the Pack—and it wasn't low. Tracy was a powerful woman, and if she'd had political aspirations, the wolves currently in leadership positions would've had to be wary. As it was, she was more interested in protecting her child, and the children of the Pack. She spoke to her father and his lieutenants on issues the Pack faced with their kids. She'd become a bit of a spokesperson for the other moms in the Pack.

She hadn't quite expected that result, but she couldn't say she was displeased with it. As a result of her work for the moms and kids in the Pack, she'd gained respect, not only from the mothers and children, but also their mates. Her status within the Pack had risen, and Tracy felt the rightness of her role as an advocate for those who were weaker than herself. She liked helping people—especially those too little to speak for themselves, or too timid because of their submissive nature.

Tracy wasn't at all submissive or weak—a fact Hank seemed to already comprehend, much to her satisfaction. Her inner wolf had always liked the way he treated her, not like some hothouse flower, but more as an equal. Even if the wolf didn't quite understand his feline intellect, it respected his power. For there was no doubt that Hank had an Alpha presence.

Tracy might still be confused about his role in his Clan, but there was no denying his dominance. In a battle of wills, she would be hard pressed to pick a winner between the two of them. She hoped he never put her in that kind of position, because more and more, she was realizing it would hurt something deep inside to have to fight him.

That's why she was hoping to keep this as civilized as possible between them. She knew she'd done wrong in not telling him about Emma, but she wasn't going to back down if he tried to take her baby away. There had to be some kind of compromise they could reach, that would leave them both happy and Emma safe with the love and caring of both her parents. Tracy just didn't know what that compromise might look like yet.

She knew she had to talk to Hank to hammer out an agreement. Hence, her bold move in sitting down at his table uninvited. He didn't seem at all displeased by her presence, though, so she took heart. Maybe this would all work out, somehow.

"Would you like to join me for lunch?" Hank asked politely.

"I've already eaten, thanks," she told him, then forged ahead. "We need to iron a few things out regarding Emma, and I think we should try to work on that tonight. Join us for dinner, and we can talk after Em goes to bed." She gave him a stern look. "Just talk."

"If that's what you want," Hank said, not looking entirely happy but committed nonetheless. "Can I come early again, to spend a little time with Emma?"

"If you wish," she told him, standing as the young waitress returned with his food. Tracy left the table without saying more.

It was hard to see him after what they'd shared the night

before. She had a definite weak spot for him and had regretted giving in to her need for him as soon as her passion had cooled.

He'd been so good to her. So solicitous of her. He was such a charmer. But it wasn't just charm. No, he really cared. She could feel it in his every touch, his every kiss.

It was incredibly seductive. She could easily come to believe in the fairytale and start thinking about things that she really couldn't have. Better to set ground rules now, and not violate them again.

She had to be strong and resist his devastating charm.

Hank had a plan. He was going to lay siege to his lady's heart and convince her—seduce her—into agreeing to visit Jaguar Island. He was reasonably certain that once she saw all the advantages Emma would have there, Tracy would agree to some kind of joint parenting. More than that, though, he wanted desperately to convince her to live with him and be his mate in truth.

He wanted that more than he wanted his next breath. She was so incredibly special to him. How could she not see that already? Hank's deepest fear was that Tracy didn't feel the same way about him as he felt about her. But that went against everything he'd ever heard about true mates.

He wanted so desperately to believe that she was his true mate. He felt it. He couldn't ascribe the feelings inside him to anything else. Yet, if he was feeling it, she should be too, right?

But what if she didn't? What if he was—impossibly—wrong? What if he was deluding himself because he wanted a mate of his own so badly?

No. He couldn't let doubt cripple him. He had a plan, and he was going to stick to it.

Tracy wouldn't know what hit her.

That's why, later, when they'd put Emma to bed, Hank didn't give her a chance to talk. He knew she might see his seduction as a bit of a betrayal. After all, he'd come here under the pretense of having some kind of serious talk about Emma's future, but he was a cat. They were known to be sneaky. Tracy knew that as well as anyone.

When he turned on the charm and made a move, she didn't do much protesting. In fact, she didn't do any protesting at all. She melted into his arms as if that's where she wanted to be for always and ever.

Hank didn't hesitate. He made love to his mate, trying to show her without words how good they could be together. How perfect.

He caressed her every curve with hands, lips and tongue. He made her pant. He made her sweat. He made her bite and growl softly, knowing she didn't dare make too much noise while Emma was asleep in the house.

This time, he carried Tracy up to her bedroom, shutting them behind the locked door, just in case the little one woke up. If Emma did wake up and climb out of her bed, they'd hear it on the baby monitor Tracy kept at her bedside.

He laid Tracy on the bed and set about proving his undying affection for his mate. He worshipped her body, showing her in practical terms how much he valued her spirit. He'd been a fool for too long. Now that he had Tracy in his arms again, he wasn't going to waste any more time trying to convince her that he really did care for her. That she really was his mate.

Tracy was having a hard time catching her breath as Hank kept her off balance both physically and mentally. He knew just where and how to touch her to send her senses into orbit, and it wasn't long before she was tearing at his clothing, wanting to touch his skin.

Hank obliged, undressing them both with quiet efficiency, all the while keeping up his unrelenting assault on her senses, touching, licking and caressing her into a frenzy of need. Damn. He was good. Better than good. He was fantastic!

When he flipped her to lay face down on the bed, she wanted to howl in delight but didn't dare make a sound. He was appealing to her inner animal, this time, lifting her ass in the air and moving behind her. Doggy style, they called it. She wouldn't have expected it so easily from a cat, and the silly thought made her smile, even as Hank's hard cock sank into her from behind.

Oh, yeah. That's what she wanted. Right…there.

He started slow then began to increase his pace as she shut her eyes and just enjoyed. Damn. That felt good.

He'd used a condom again. Thoughtful kitty. Just for that, she'd lick him later. As her thoughts turned slightly scandalous, Hank began to move faster. The pressure built until it exploded outward in a geyser of ecstasy that stole her breath and made her want to howl.

She didn't. Ever conscious of the little person sleeping next door, Tracy growled into the pillow beneath her head as pleasure racked her willing body. She felt Hank stiffen and heard a low, feline growl escape his throat. Sexy.

He let her down slowly and then lay at her side in the aftermath, holding her close. When his chest started vibrating with a purring sound, she smiled and placed her hand over his heart. She'd never been with a man who purred before…except Hank. Only Hank had ever shown her how sexy a cat could be.

CHAPTER 11

"You know, I really thought I meant what I said when I invited you over here just to talk," Tracy mused as she lay spooned against Hank's warm body deep in the night, after their third round of lovemaking.

"You think differently now?" he asked, his voice dropping into that purring growl that made her insides tremble with desire. Her pussy cat was just too damned sexy.

"Apparently, I was lying to myself as much as you." She turned so she could face him but stayed close. "I'm sorry, Hank. I've been very confused since you came back. I know that's not really an excuse, but it's the truth."

He stroked her hair back from her face with one hand. "That's okay. This is a confusing situation. I'm sorry I didn't realize you were..." He stopped talking, his expression growing shuttered.

"Were what?" she asked, suspicious about what he had been going to say.

Hank seemed to come to a decision. "I've been kicking myself ten ways to Sunday about this, sweetheart. Somehow, I didn't realize you were my true, Goddess-given mate."

"Mate," she tested the word as if weighing how it felt in her mouth. "You seriously think so?"

Hank nodded solemnly. "I know it's a lot to take in. It was

for me, too. But I truly believe that's what we've been fighting. We were always meant to be together. Emma is proof of that, if we need any more."

"But you're a cat!" She hadn't meant to say it. It just came out.

Hank chuckled. "I know. Terrible of me, isn't it? Ruining all your preconceived ideas about the wolf you'd end up with. If it makes any difference, you blew up all my expectations too."

Her first instinct was to bite him. How dare he laugh about something so serious? Then, she stopped to think about what he'd said and realized he was right—about her expectations, at least. She still wasn't buying into the true mate hypothesis.

"I'm not so sure about the mate thing, but I will admit I'm more attracted to you than I've ever been to anyone else. If that means mating…" She thought about it for a moment more and was glad he didn't rush her. "I'm not prepared to go that far…yet. I always thought there would be sparkling lights and fairies singing or something," she admitted, laughing at her own childish ideas. "I'm going to have to think about this."

"I wouldn't expect anything less of my pensive…" He placed a quick kiss on her forehead. "Pedantic…" He kissed the tip of her nose. "Passionate…" This time, he kissed her lips and lingered. "Pretty, pretty mate," he whispered after he let her up for air.

She let the claim slide this time. She liked the way he complimented her. He knew just how to stroke her inner wolf, and her human sensibilities, as well.

"Will you come to the island to visit?" he asked after a short lull where they just held each other quietly. "I can fly you back with me and then bring you back here whenever you want."

Tracy sighed. "Was that what this was all about? You were seducing me into agreeing to visit the island?"

He shrugged. "Did it work?"

"You're incorrigible," she told him, smiling despite herself. He really was a charming rogue.

She'd already given the idea of visiting the island a lot of thought and realized it wouldn't be fair to Emma if she didn't at least try to see how the jaguars lived. She'd already half-decided to go back with him when he left—just for a short stay. Did she let him think he'd seduced her into it, or did she make it clear she had already mostly decided to go anyway?

What difference did it really make? It seemed petty now, to try to belabor the point, so she just smiled at him.

"We'll go with you," she told him, gratified when his face lit up with happiness. He was devastating when he was serious, but he was incredible when he smiled. Her tummy lurched with the attraction that never seemed to fade. "Just for a short visit, though," she qualified, trying to be stern.

His joy didn't dim with her harsher tone. He leaned in and kissed her soundly, then drew back, meeting her gaze. "Thank you, Tracy. I can't wait to show you my home."

When they arrived the next day—for Hank hadn't wasted any time getting Tracy and Emma on his plane once she'd agreed to go—Jaguar Island was like nothing Tracy could have imagined. An island paradise, for sure, but it still looked so wild and untamed. Yet, she was sure she'd heard the jaguars all lived there.

"There's only one house," she mused as they got off the plane and she had her first good look around. "Does everyone live in that mansion? I mean, everybody knows the jaguars suffered greatly and were diminished in numbers, but I really thought there were more of you than that."

Hank chuckled as he picked up Emma and carried her down the short staircase that led from the cabin of the plane to the tarmac. He kissed her on the cheek before setting her back on her little feet.

"Cats are really good at stealth," he told her. "The mansion was here when Mark bought the place. It serves its purpose as camouflage, and a place to bring the occasional non-Clan guest."

"Will we be staying there?" Tracy bent down to pick up Emma while Pax and Ari handled the bags for them. The two giant jaguars had turned out to be nice guys and had kept both Tracy and Emma entertained on the long plane ride.

"If you want to," Hank said as they began walking up the winding shell-lined path that led to the mansion. "But I'd hoped you'd stay at my place. There's plenty of room."

Tracy wondered if he expected her to share his bed if she stayed with him. If possible, she'd try to see the accommodations offered by both choices before making a decision. She had to choose what was best for Em, even if Tracy's hormones wanted to share sexy Hank's bed again. And again. And again.

Down, girl.

Hank was nervous introducing Tracy to Mark and the rest of his people. Would she like them? Would they like her? It was strange to be introducing a werewolf onto the island—a place designed for cats. Even now, Hank spotted a few of his Clan mates in the trees, watching the path. They were holding back, for now, not sure what to make of the mother and child.

For, it was obvious to anyone who scented them that Tracy was Emma's mother, yet their inner animals were completely different. It happened, but not often, that mates were of different species. Cats had been known to mate bear shifters in the past—both species liked to roam alone, so that sort of made sense—but Hank didn't know of any other wolf-jaguar matches. Wolves wanted to constantly be surrounded by Pack. Jaguars? Not so much.

In fact, that was one of the potential problems in asking Pax and Ari here. They were protectors of their own small Clan in Arizona, but here, they would be surrounded by a lot more jaguars with a lot less real estate. Clashes could happen.

Hank didn't flinch when a very large jaguar jumped out of a tree on the path in front of them. Tracy reflexively held

Emma tighter, Hank noted, but he knew the male cat that had just put on a display, and Hank suspected it was more for Pax and Ari's benefit than Tracy's.

"Knock it off, Mario. You're scaring my daughter," Hank said, figuring little Emma would forgive him for the face-saving falsehood.

Emma was far from frightened by the big cat's appearance. In fact, she was peering with wide eyes from her mother's hold, noting everything about the new feline. It was Tracy that was apprehensive, as any protective mother should be in new and unknown situation. Hank moved closer to her and put one hand on her shoulder.

"Don't mind him. He's probably here to check out our other guests," Hank murmured to Tracy as Mario paused, nodded once, then moved past them with a swish of his tail. Sure enough, he walked right up to Pax and growled.

Pax growled back, but Hank knew they were growls of greeting. Friendly sounds. Apparently, Mario knew these guys.

"Don't let ol' Mario spook you, Miss Tracy," Ari offered from the rear of the small party. "We worked with him a few years back. He just came to say hello, now that we're in his home territory."

Hank resumed walking, escorting Tracy and Emma while Pax, Ari and Mario spaced themselves a few yards behind. It felt good to walk on the island with Tracy beside him. Having her here was something he'd never expected but had started to want with all his heart. He hoped she liked the place enough to consider visiting with Emma from time to time, but he was concerned her inner wolf would be driven up the wall being surrounded by cats.

"I'm sorry about the long walk. We left it this way deliberately," Hank told Tracy. "Another layer of security. We get to see everyone who comes up this path from multiple angles."

"And of course you have people in the trees," she said, nodding toward where another jaguar lounged in the crook of a forked tree trunk.

"Well spotted," he complimented her skill in seeing the golden jaguar against the dappled sunlight in the trees.

Tracy tapped her nose and smiled softly. "The nose always knows," she told him.

"We should have a smell-off sometime," he mused aloud.

"A what?" She looked at him, humor dancing in her eyes.

"You heard me. I've always wondered if wolves had more sensitive noses than jaguars. We could test it." They rounded the final bend, at that point, and the house was before them.

Tracy didn't answer as little Emma demanded to be put down, only so she could run straight for the porch of the mansion where a young couple was sitting in the shade, tall glasses of lemonade on a table between them. Hank held his breath. Mark and his mate were waiting for them.

And like all good little jaguars, Emma recognized the Alpha and wanted to be near him. Damn. That just about choked Hank up, realizing his daughter—his *daughter*—was about to meet their Clan leader. Hank had never really thought this day would come, and yet, somehow, the Mother of All had been smiling down on him.

She was probably chuckling right now, as a matter of fact. If the Goddess had put Hank and Tracy together in the first place, which he now believed had been the case, then She was no doubt frustrated at how stupid he'd been not to recognize his mate for so very long.

Hank vowed to make up for the lost time. He'd figure a way.

Tracy hesitated, and Hank put his hand on her arm. "She'll be fine. Her jaguar recognizes its Alpha, that's all. Mark would sooner bite off his own hand than hurt a baby."

Hank murmured the comforting words near Tracy's ear as they continued toward the house, Emma racing ahead on her chubby little legs. She was wearing the cutest sundress today, with a colorful cartoon lion's head on the front. She made it to the stairs that led up to where Mark and Shelly were sitting, and that slowed her down, but Emma was determined. On hands and knees, she made her way up the three wide steps and then made a beeline for Mark.

By the time Emma reached the Alpha jaguar, Hank and Tracy were mounting the steps. Mark caught Emma and lifted her to sit on his lap.

"And who's this?" he asked the child, who giggled, content in the Alpha's protective presence.

"Mark." Hank cleared his suddenly tight throat and tried again. "Alpha. This is Emma. My daughter." Hank felt pride swell in his chest as he presented his offspring to the Alpha, but he had another duty—equally special—to perform. "And this is her mother, Tracy Villalobos."

Mark stood, carrying Emma easily, to face Hank and Tracy. His eyes went golden as his inner jaguar shone through.

"I'm very pleased to meet you, Alpha," Tracy said, not lowering her head or showing any sign of submissiveness. Hank had to smile. That was his pretty mate. Fierce and protective of her baby. Tracy wouldn't let a mere billionaire Alpha predator intimidate her.

"Likewise, Miss Villalobos. I've been speaking with your father. Good man. Good Alpha to his people," Mark commented before turning his attention back to Emma, who was walking her little fingers up his shirt. Little fingers with little claws.

Mark took one of Emma's hands in his much bigger one and tapped on the claws. "No scratching, kitten, okay?" Emma looked up into the Alpha's eyes and nodded solemnly.

"No hurt," she said, agreeing to the Alpha's admonition.

"She can do partial shifts already?" Mark commented, looking at Hank with a knowing grin. "You'd better watch out. She is one strong little jaguar."

Emma gave her new Alpha a cute growl that sounded adorable. Mark chuckled and passed the child to her mother's arms.

"Miss Villalobos—Tracy—this is my mate, Shelly," Mark introduced the woman who had stood and come to his side.

Shelly waved to Emma, who was opening and closing one little fist in her version of hello.

"Hi," Shelly said, smiling kindly. "Welcome to the island. I hope you'll enjoy your stay."

Tracy knew right off that Shelly wasn't a shifter. She had the scent of magic about her, but no animal spirit that Tracy could discern. Curious. One of the most powerful Alphas in the world was mated to a human? Tracy wondered if Shelly was a mage. That might explain it. Otherwise, the pairing seemed like a bit of a mismatch.

An Alpha with the reputation, fame and fortune of Mark Pepard should, by all rights, have an equally powerful mate. There had to be more to Shelly than was readily visible. Either that—or Pepard was into total domination. In which case, Tracy would want nothing to do with him. She'd give it time for the truth to reveal itself, but she'd keep her eyes open.

"Would you like some lemonade?" Shelly went on, inviting Tracy to sit with a gesture. Tracy agreed and sat on the other side of the small table from the Alpha pair, with Emma still on her lap. Hank and Mark sat, too.

Shelly did the honors, pouring out lemonade for the adults and procuring a sippy cup with apple juice for Emma, showing she'd prepared for their arrival. The extra thought touched Tracy, who thanked their hostess with a friendly smile.

"We have quite a few cubs that like to visit," Shelly told Tracy. "I like to be prepared for little guests, as well as their guardians."

"That's very thoughtful and much appreciated," Tracy replied as Emma drank down the juice which was in a plastic cup decorated with her favorite cartoon princesses. "Have you lived here long?"

"Not too long," Shelly answered. "I feel like we're still in our honeymoon phase," she said with a smile for her mate as she took his hand.

"Shelly's definitely putting her mark on the island, though," Mark told her with a hint of pride. "My mate is a brilliant architect, and she's been designing community buildings and homes for the entire island."

"That sounds both impressive and ambitious," Tracy answered with a grin.

She couldn't say why, exactly, but she had an instant liking for Shelly. Mark seemed all right too, though she was still a bit in awe of him, privately. It wasn't every day she met a billionaire Alpha with the clout to buy and sell her family's airport—which was a big operation, itself—twenty times over.

"He won't let me change the mansion too much, though," Shelly said as she nudged her mate with a friendly elbow. "I could do wonders with this place. It has good bones, but the look is really dated."

Tracy tilted her head to one side as if considering. "It's not bad if you like the early massive white box style."

"Oh, don't forget the columns! Early massive Greek revival white box," Shelly put in, laughing freely. One thing was certain—this Alpha female was happy with her position here, and her mate. That much was obvious, though Tracy would still watch for any signs of discontent.

The Alpha pair set the tone for the entire Pack—or Clan, in this case. If they were happy, generally their people were, too. And, if they had a good partnership in their mating, their Clan members often followed their example. The Alpha pair were the template for the rest of the group, or so her father had said many, many times.

Which was part of why he'd been so dog-gone mad at Tracy for having a baby without a father. What kind of example had she been holding up for the rest of the Pack? Not that there was anything wrong with having a baby. Her father doted on Emma. But the precedent of not mating and having what he considered a stable family life for her daughter was what got to him.

Tracy had tried to show him that she could be both

mother and father to Emma and had done really well until her daughter had gone all kitty cat on her. Tracy didn't know how to deal with a growing cat shifter. She was out of her depth there, and she knew it. In order for Emma to have the best start possible with her life as a shifter and her spirit animal's comfort, she needed the presence of other jaguars. That was one of the main reasons Tracy was here. Emma needed to be around jaguars, and these were her extended family. Her Clan.

If Tracy could assure that Emma would have a place among these people, this Clan, then she would have done a really good thing to ensure her daughter's future success as a person and as a jaguar. Tracy knew that, and though her inner wolf was a bit itchy around all these cats, the Alpha bitch inside her knew they had to do this for their baby. Protecting her child was something both halves of her nature understood and would go to any lengths to accomplish.

Tracy let go such serious thoughts and turned mentally back to their silly conversation. "I like this porch, though. I can just imagine sitting out here at night, watching the harbor below."

"Yeah, it's really pretty," Shelly agreed. "There's not a lot of boat traffic, except for our own, of course, but we can see tankers, container vessels, and the odd cruise ship in the distance. There's a major shipping route not too far away, so there's usually something lit up out there at night."

"Sounds magical," Tracy admitted. "Where I'm from in Northern Texas, we're landlocked. Closest we come to a big body of water is Big Wolf Lake."

"Is the town named for the lake or the lake for the town?" Hank asked, his blue eyes glinting at her in merriment.

"Now, you know my father well enough by now to understand that everything in the area is named for the Pack. Big Wolf, Texas, supports Big Wolf Airport, encompasses Big Wolf Lake, the Big Wolf Golf Course, Big Wolf Hunt Club—which is not really what it sounds like because there are no humans allowed—and a number of other businesses and locations all named after the Pack. We kid Dad that he had no imagination when he named everything, but he just smiles and looks over his empire with a sort of satisfied grin."

Mark folded his hands over his middle and leaned back in his chair as if surveying his domain. "Nothing wrong with that," was his wry comment, which made everyone chuckle.

"Says the man who renamed an entire island," Shelly put in. "After his Clan."

"What was it called before?" Tracy asked out of curiosity.

"Paradise Cove," Shelly answered.

"Sounded a little too swinging singles to me," Mark said, a small scowl on his handsome face. "This place is for families. Jaguar families."

"And the occasional wolf," Hank added, putting his hand over Tracy's.

Mark nodded. "The occasional wolf, human, mage, and whoever else the Mother of All wants us to add to our merry band of jaguars," he agreed. "I know it's not the same for wolves, but jaguars seldom mate each other. Throughout our history, we've usually chosen mates from other groups. You won't find any problems here, except maybe that our Clan mates will be curious about your animal. We get a lot of other kinds of cats when our people mate other shifters, but you'll be the first wolf in my lifetime."

"She can handle it," Hank assured his Alpha before Tracy could say anything. She liked that Hank had confidence in her, but she was intrigued by Mark's choice of words.

"Do you have records of other wolves being involved with jaguars?" she asked.

To her surprise, Mark nodded again. "In fact, we do. Not written records, but *Abuela* remembers a mated pair from her generation. The male was the wolf in that instance, and the female one of us. He gave up his Pack for her when his people wouldn't accept his mating and came to live with *Abuela's* familial Clan. His name was Rodrigo, and he died in the drug wars, protecting his family, as so many of our people have died. His grandson is one of the teachers in our school."

"So, all the children were jaguars?" Tracy asked after a pause to respect Rodrigo's sacrifice.

"Most," Mark said, smiling. "But *Abuela* talked about a set of twins that wound up being the South American Lords."

"Wolves! Their mother was a jaguar?" Everybody knew that both the North and South American Lords were wolves at this moment in time, which was odd because the honor rotated among the shifter Tribes, Clans and Packs, depending on which species was blessed with a set of identical male twins that survived to adulthood.

Mark nodded. "I like to think growing up jaguar made them better at what they do for all shifters in their part of the world, but of course, that was a little before my time. We're on good terms, though. They support the idea of the remaining jaguars banding together to strengthen our species."

Tracy was impressed, but then again, who else would Lords talk to but a billionaire shifter with power in both the human and shifter worlds. She had to remind herself this man wasn't just any Alpha. He was the Jaguar Alpha, which meant big things in this day and age. He'd built an empire in the human world and used it to protect and rebuild his Clan. The man was reputed to be lethal in both business and in combat, regardless of his laid back presence.

Cats were like that, sometimes. They looked all soft and fuzzy on the outside. They might even look a bit lazy to an active wolf. But when the moment to strike arrived...watch out.

"We're holding a little party later to welcome Emma and yourself to the island," Shelly told her. "If you want to freshen up or maybe put Emma down for a nap, I had a suite prepared for your use."

"That's very thoughtful. Thank you."

A few more minutes of conversation and Tracy took a sleepy Emma indoors to the promised resting place. To say the rooms were palatial would be an understatement. Shelly had escorted them and made sure they had everything they needed while Hank sorted out their luggage. He brought Emma and Tracy's bags to the room after Shelly left.

"Don't unpack too much," he cautioned her with a grin. "I'm hoping to convince you both to stay with me, remember. We'll probably have time to see my place after the party. We're holding it early in deference to the children. Emma's going to meet the other kids we have here. The hope is that she'll start friendships that will last a lifetime among her own peer group."

"That's a really great idea," Tracy mused. So far, she was impressed by the way the jaguars planned everything for the best effect. No wonder Mark Pepard had been able to build such an empire. If he gave this much attention to everything he did, there'd be no stopping him.

"Mark will be welcoming you both into the Clan officially," he told her, his expression going taut.

"So soon?" she asked, surprised. She'd thought the Alpha would take more time to get to know her first before taking such a step.

"There's no question you belong, Tracy. If only for Emma's sake. We do not separate children from their parents. Ever. And, more than that, I've already told Mark that you're my mate. Even if you never accept that, it's something I will hold in my soul for all time."

Tracy shook her head. Things were getting a little too serious. She knew she had to think about all of this soon, but she was on the point of overload between the long flight and the island. Meeting Pepard and his mate, Shelly. Too much was racing through her mind.

"Give me a little time, Hank," she told him in a quiet voice.

He immediately backed off toward the open doorway. "I'll leave you two to rest. Be ready in about two and a half hours, okay? I'll come pick you up."

With that, he left, and Tracy felt a little sad. She hadn't meant to reject him, but she knew he'd been hurt when he left. Damn. She just didn't know what to think anymore. Life was getting a little too complicated, but she'd have to figure it out. Somehow.

CHAPTER 12

As soon as Emma and Tracy were settled, Hank went inside to find Mark and Nick, who was head of security for the entire Clan, as expected. Mario and a few others who were much lower in the Clan hierarchy, but had been included for some reason, were also present and already in discussion with Pax and Ari. They'd arrayed themselves around a table with the brothers and Mario on one side, everyone else on the other. Not an auspicious start.

Hank went in and deliberately sat down next to the brothers, nodding to Mario as he did so. Everyone was in human form for this meeting, and Mario had shifted, grabbing some sweats that were kept on hand for anyone wanting to prowl around the jungle then shift when they got to the mansion.

Mario had worked with the two brothers in the past. Hank was a new champion of the fraternal twin Master Chiefs, but he was definitely in favor of Pax and Ari joining the bigger Clan. They were good men who had a lot to offer. Hank wanted to make sure they were given the opportunity to share their gifts on a larger stage.

The meeting went on for a long time. Pax started out belligerent, and then, he switched off with his twin. It was almost like a game to them. They even referenced the seating arrangements—the subtleties not being lost on the twins, who gave every appearance of being big muscle jocks with not much in the brain department. Hank had learned the two cultivated that impression and were actually using it to their advantage whenever possible. There were deep thinking minds inside those supposedly empty skulls, and the rest of the Clan needed to figure that out.

Tensions were running high as the brothers stonewalled the younger Clan members, who were the only ones speaking so far. Hank sat back and watched the twins play the game. Mario kept quiet, but he seemed concerned. The folks arrayed across the table were rising to the bait Pax and Ari kept throwing out—all except for Mark and Nick, who were also sitting back and watching events unfold.

Good. At least Hank could count on those two not to be taken in by the ruse. They were the real leaders of the Jaguar Clan. Mark had the much more public role of Alpha, but Jaguars ran things a little differently than most other shifters. Nick, as head of security—a modern name for an ancient position—had as much authority in his area of responsibility, but none of the public scrutiny.

"I don't think we can work with these people, do you, Pax?" Ari said to his twin. Things had come to a head according to the brothers' game plan. Hank was glad. Maybe now, if they could get past this turning point, they might actually accomplish something.

"If you two have finished playing games..." Hank said, throwing a wadded up piece of paper at Ari, which he batted easily aside.

Both twins turned exasperated expressions on Hank. "Why are you spoiling the fun, man?" Pax asked, disbelief written all over his face.

"You know I like a good prank better than most of you," Hank said. "But you're not fooling them, guys. At least not Nick and Mark. They see right through you, so you want to stop baiting the gullible and finally get down to business? I've got a party to get ready for, and I want to look my best so I can convince a certain stubborn wolf that she belongs with me forever."

Ari grinned. "Well, when you put it that way."

Pax shook his head. "Sorry, Hank. You know we just like yanking their chains. And you guys..." Pax pointed to the men flanking Nick and Mark on the other side of the table. "You made it too easy. You gonna need to look deeper at what's in front of you if we are supposed to work together."

"Is that possible?" Nick asked, speaking for the first time. "You see the problems I've got here. I brought these guys along, because they're not very senior, and I wanted them to get a little experience, but they've failed the test." Chagrinned cat shifters now hung their heads on either side of Nick and Mark. "But they'll learn...if they have good teachers and examples. I think that's a role you two could fulfill, if you're willing."

Hank saw Mario relax and the younger cats shut up while the leadership got down to brass tacks. Pax and Ari were a lot more reasonable when speaking with Mark and Nick, now that all the posturing had been put aside.

Hank left before all the I's were dotted and T's crossed, but he was confident that he'd done his part to get the negotiations onto the right footing. As he'd told the others, he had to get ready for the party, and he wanted to run over to his house and make sure it was presentable. After the party, he planned to take his mate and daughter home for the first time, and he really wanted them to stay...forever, if possible.

The party later that day was wonderful. There were a lot more baby jaguars on the island than Tracy had expected, and Emma didn't lack for playmates around her own age. The other moms made Tracy feel at home as they discussed the ups and downs of having babies that shifted at such a young age.

The first few moments of the gathering were a little uncomfortable for Tracy. Mark and Shelly asked her to bring

Emma up front to where Hank was already waiting, next to the Alpha pair. Then, Mark made a formal introduction of both Tracy and her baby to the gathered Clan members. There was a brief moment of silence while everybody looked them over—or so it seemed to Tracy—before a cheer went up and folks came forward to be introduced one at a time, or in family groups.

Actually, the families were the easiest to handle. As they came forward and the children met each other, the adults found common ground. When enough little ones had met Emma, an older woman everyone called *Abuela* took them all to a quiet corner that was set up for the children with padding on the hardwood floor and plush toys to play with. Tracy was convinced to let Emma join the other children in that area under the grandmotherly woman's supervision, though Tracy made sure to keep Emma in sight at all times. Her inner wolf would've gone a little crazy in this house full of cats if it couldn't see her baby.

The others seemed to understand, and a clear line of sight was left between the parents and the play area. The single cats came over to meet Tracy, once she had staked out her little area from which to watch Emma. Hank stayed by her side and introduced everyone. She wasn't surprised by the way they treated him. Universally, Hank made everyone smile, but they also respected him. It was clear in the way the younger ones deferred to him and how those of his own generation spoke with him as an equal.

Hank might be an easygoing joker on the outside, but his Clan knew he was a capable man when it was necessary. They counted on him. Even Mark Pepard seemed to see Hank as a trusted aide, and Tracy wondered again about Hank's exact place in the hierarchy. He was of an even higher rank than she'd thought, as she watched him interact with his Alpha. They were more like friends than Alpha and subordinate.

In fact, seeing Hank's close relationship with the Clan and with Mark made her accept more of what he'd tried to tell her before about how much the Alpha and the Clan depended on him. It was easier to accept that he truly had been working hard for his people for the years they'd been apart. And, it made sense that loveable, affable, skilled Hank had been the go-to guy for whatever the Clan had needed of him. He just had a generous heart, a unique set of skills, and an easy-going disposition that made him a natural leader among his people.

Tracy was impressed with the way Mark dealt with everyone, too. They all respected him, it was clear to see, but they also seemed to genuinely love him. Alphas each had their own style of leadership. Her own father was more of a disciplinarian and a father figure to the entire Pack. Mark was more of a friend. He acted like everybody's older brother. Make that everybody's *very protective* older brother. She had no doubt he would come to the rescue of any one of these cats, when needed.

And it seemed like they would do the same for him. To be loved so well by one's Clan was a gift, indeed. Most Alphas never quite achieved this kind of unity, though the good ones tried. At least, according to her father.

She had a good basis for comparison having grown up watching Joe Villalobos build his empire from the ground up. He'd done it with compassion and love, not intimidation. Though he was the baddest wolf in town, he never abused his power over the rest of the Pack. He'd created something for them all to share. He'd put the Big Wolf Pack on the map, both literally and figuratively. They had a town, an airport and countless businesses that now supported a growing and healthy Pack. All due to her father's vision and the hard work of both him and the rest of the Pack.

It looked like Mark was trying to do something similar here. Only, being jaguars, they were doing it in a much more exotic way. Tracy had to shake her head. Who, other than a billionaire cat with extravagant spots, would buy an entire island? Mark didn't seem to know the meaning of the word *subtle*.

Then again, that might just be part of his game. Cats were sneaky, and while he'd done something showy here, in buying a whole freaking island, he was also secretive enough to keep all but specifically invited guests from coming here. He wasn't trying to rebuild his Clan on the mainland, where they would have to deal with the human world every day. No, he'd built a sanctuary where jaguars could be jaguars, in peace and with a high expectation of privacy.

Knowing that, and having met Mark and his mate, Tracy was growing a lot more curious to see the rest of the island— the inner sanctum Shelly had hinted at when describing her architectural designs. It sure sounded a lot different than the public façade presented by the old-style mansion.

By the time the party ended, after a light buffet had been served and consumed and the smaller children began to feel sleepy, Tracy was ready to see Hank's home. She knew he'd been wanting to show her his place, and she had agreed already to go there after the party. Talking about the island and the different amenities already in place for families with children, Tracy was even more intrigued.

They left the mansion together, Hank carrying a sleepy Emma in his arms. Tracy had brought along a bag with essentials but had opted to leave their suitcases in the suite they'd been given in the mansion. Still, she always brought an extra set of clothing with her for Emma. If she shifted and destroyed what she was wearing, it was always good to have a backup.

Throwing an extra set of underwear in the bag for herself was something she didn't want to think too much about. Perhaps she was already planning to stay the night in her subconscious mind. Maybe she just wanted to be prepared for anything. Either way, she wasn't going to examine her motives too closely.

They took an all-terrain vehicle with big tires as far as they could, but all Tracy saw was jungle. The leafy canopy hid the trail from above, she realized, as the light grew dim. It wasn't quite sundown in this part of the world yet, but it was coming on fast. Faster, under the cover of the giant trees all around.

"We have to walk from here," Hank told Tracy as he

parked the vehicle under a tree.

She noted several other similar vehicles parked all around, camouflaged by the greenery. They had driven steadily higher, but with all the foliage, she hadn't really been able to get a sense of where they were in relation to the long-dormant volcano that was at the core of the island.

There were a few faint trails leading from the parking area that only her sharp wolf senses allowed her to pick out. These cats were crafty. They weren't blazing any trails that could be seen from the air or easily followed even on the ground.

"You all use different paths to get to your territory?" Tracy asked, trying to figure out how they worked it.

"We all have a slice of territory to call our own," Hank told her gently. "Mark worked it out so each of us have our own home territory. It helps settle our cats to have a defined area to patrol."

"Each wolf family has their own small territory around their homes, but it sounds like you're talking about something a lot bigger than a backyard," Tracy commented.

Hank chuckled. "Wolves like togetherness from what I've observed. We're a bit different. We each need our own space. Not just a house or a yard, but a defined area that is ours alone." He guided her through the undergrowth, politely holding back an overhanging limb for her as she carried Emma in her arms. "There's a reason your people gather in Packs and we prefer a Clan structure. We're not quite as social as wolves, but we're learning to peacefully coexist here. Mark's making it happen, and we're all dedicated to the project, because we've lost so many of our kind by being stubborn lone operators. We're rebuilding. Together."

Tracy knew a bit of the history of the decline of the jaguar people. Her father had talked to her about what he knew while Hank was in Arizona. Her heart went out to all those lone jaguar families who had failed to defend their jungle homes from gangs of humans with guns and a thirst for drug dollars. It was a tragedy, but she was impressed all over again at the way Mark had rallied his remaining people to not only survive, but thrive, even if they had to adapt to a new way of living to do it.

"See this?" Hank paused by a large tree and pointed to a set of claw marks. "This is my mark," he told her. "To us, the claw marks denote each jaguar's territory. We choose our marks when we come of age. In my case, it's four stripes, about four inches long. Of course, each set of claws makes a slightly different mark, and we all know each other's prints, even without the chosen mark, but this is the official seal, if you will. The mark of my boundary line. Once we pass this point, we're in my territory."

"I'm guessing the depth of the marks and the pressure used is something you can differentiate as well?" Tracy asked, running her finger alongside the outermost gouge. She was familiar with paw prints and claw marks, but her people didn't use them as extensively as the cats seemed to do.

Hank smiled at her. "You bet," he replied. "Jaguars are creatures of subtlety. It's good you realize that since you're raising one. You might have to read between the lines with Emma once she gets older and starts growing into her jaguar spirit. She won't always tell you what's wrong. Jaguar parents often complain of having to be detectives to figure out what's bugging their kids sometimes. But it's a sort of game—even though the stakes are high—and we cats love games, as much as we love our children. Cats love figuring out puzzles."

"Wolves are pretty good at puzzles too," Tracy claimed, smiling as they moved on. She stepped over the invisible boundary into his territory, feeling as if she'd just taken a step into her future. One she might live to regret, but hoped and prayed would turn out all right for both her and her daughter.

"That's good," Hank told her, his demeanor changing now that they were in his territory. He seemed to examine every tree, every leaf, pride showing in his expression, but also alertness. "Nobody on the island would breach my territory without express invitation," he told her as they walked deeper into the forest. "Except maybe *Abuela*. She goes where she wants, and something tells me she's been through here recently." A sort of puzzled smile lit his face as they moved forward.

"Whose grandmother is she?" Tracy asked, knowing the word was Spanish for grandmother.

"Nick's, actually, but she's more or less the entire Clan's granny and guardian angel rolled into one. She's a wise woman. She counsels us all when we need it, and she's always there if we need to talk. She's a treasure the entire Clan cherishes."

"I can tell. Whenever she's mentioned, it's with love," Tracy observed. She liked that this Clan of loners had a communal grandmother to nurture them.

"There were some little cats through here too, with her," Hank said, pointing to little human footprints in a bare spot of dirt. Tiny sneakers with distinctive treads. More than one pair. "What in the world was she doing up here with the kids?"

They walked a little farther, and suddenly, the dense undergrowth opened into a small clearing where a structure was nestled against the side of the curved wall of the crater. It was hidden from above by the rock and the towering trees that had been left in strategic places. The structure was brown and green, made of materials that blended into the surroundings beautifully. And the front door was festooned with flowers. Somehow, Tracy didn't think Hank had planted those on his own.

"I think you have your answer as to what *Abuela* and the children were doing up here. Unless you're a fan of purple and pink pansies." Tracy chuckled at the haphazardly planted flowers. She could just picture enthusiastic little hands patting the soil in the pots that had been put on either side of the doorway.

"That's to welcome you and Emma," Hank said, clearing his throat. "I certainly never planted any flowers around my house.

"That's so sweet," Tracy said, letting Emma down so she could take a closer look at the colorful display. Tracy stood and took a good look at the structure. "It's a lovely house, Hank."

"Thanks." Was he blushing? He certainly seemed subdued for a man who usually shone so bright. "Shelly designed it," he went on, but she suspected there was more to the construction that he wasn't telling.

"You helped, didn't you?" she prodded, wanting to know more.

"I came up with some of the ideas, and I did a lot of the labor myself, in between assignments. We changed a few things from the original design as we were working, but Shelly approved everything," he was quick to point out. "It's all safe and structurally sound. We have a building team here on the island that has lots of experience on the mainland. They know their trades inside and out, and they work on, or supervise, every structure we put up, so we're sure everything we build is completely safe."

"That's impressive," she told him, wanting to reassure him that she wasn't questioning his abilities or the safety of his home. "My dad does something similar, but of course, we all help each other with everything anyway. If something needs repair or building from the ground up, all the folks who have experience always chip in, so there's no question things get done the right way."

"Pack life sounds kind of nice, though a bit intrusive," he observed.

She chuckled. "To tell you the truth, all the togetherness can get to me sometimes. You wouldn't believe the busybodies who came out of the woodwork when Emma started shifting. I actually told everybody off at a Pack meeting and was later chastised by my dad for hurting their feelings when they were only trying to be neighborly." She gave a long sigh. "Pack is great, but it can get on my nerves occasionally."

"Maybe your feline daughter is rubbing off on you," Hank mused with a grin.

"Or her feline father," she agreed, bumping his arm gently

with her shoulder.

"I wouldn't mind rubbing off on you at all," he said, deviltry in his dancing eyes.

She laughed outright at his innuendo. Hank was fun to be around. Emma looked away from her intense scrutiny of the pretty flowers, laughing along with her mother, though she had no idea what was so funny.

Tracy reached out and picked Emma up, swinging her around to her delighted giggles. When she came back to where she'd started, she noticed that Hank had already opened the front door. He came over to her and picked her up in his arms, lifting both her and Emma, still clutched tight in Tracy's arms, and walked easily with them over the threshold.

He let Tracy's legs drift easily down to the floor once they were inside, but he kept one arm around her back. Tracy looked up into his eyes, and her breath caught. His gaze was smoldering, but he immediately banked the fire. Out of breath for no discernable reason, Tracy moved her gaze off him and looked around the house.

And quickly realized that the word *house* was a wholly inadequate term. The outer façade might look like a pretty little cottage in the forest, but the door opened into something quite different. The entry was open to the top of what Tracy now realized was a really large cave-like structure that went back into the rock of the volcanic rim.

"This is amazing," she breathed, nearly overcome by the imaginative design of something that was more like a den than a human house, yet had all the comforts of modern life. She could see gleaming countertops and a kitchen area in the open-concept front space. Comfy furniture in rich earth tones and jewel colors were up front in what would have been the living room in her house.

There was a big screen TV that was probably the largest she'd ever seen, and off to one side, there was a computer setup that looked like something out of a science fiction movie. A dining table was adjacent to the kitchen and looked out through the front windows she'd seen from outside. The wall at the back of the public area of the house had a couple of doors, beyond which she imagined were at least one bedroom and a bathroom, but judging by the proportions of what she could see so far, it might contain a lot more than that.

"I've been adding on as time allows," Hank said, coming up behind her. She'd moved into the large open space without thinking about it. "The private areas of the house can be locked down." He nodded toward the doorway on the right. "The left door is a bathroom for this part of the house. Once you go through the right door, you're fully inside the rock wall of the mountain."

"Don't you mean the caldera? This is the inside curve of the volcano, isn't it?" She felt a little note of concern at being inside something that had blown up a million years ago.

"*Dormant* volcano," he told her. "And besides, Mark would know if the volcano was going to be a problem. He's…sort of…connected to it, in a way. We all are, to some degree, but he's the Big Kahuna. He'd know if it was going to turn on us." Hank fell silent for a moment as she walked deeper into the living room area. "It's not, by the way. It nurtures us, not…the other thing."

Tracy looked at him, and he was gesturing with his glance toward Emma, who was watching everything with wide eyes. Tracy hugged her baby, offering reassurance in this strange place, but Emma seemed fine. Thanks in part, she was sure, to Hank's careful wording. Emma was very empathic. She always picked up on the mood of those around her, and if Tracy was afraid, Emma would be too.

"So, this is the more or less public part of the house. I sometimes have friends over to watch games, though I haven't been home much in recent years." He pointed toward the giant TV as he led the way toward the doorway that led to the back of the house. "This partition is steel plate. Nothing gets through here without some serious effort," he said with a grin as he unlocked and opened the large doorway.

Tracy could see that the door wasn't just a wooden panel. No, this door was made of metal, and it was really thick. Likewise, the lock looked heavy duty. More like a bank vault lock than a door lock.

"You expecting a siege?" she asked, only half joking. This was some serious defensive stuff. Wolves didn't build like this. Then again, werewolves, as a species, hadn't been decimated, almost to extinction.

"Not expecting," he told her, shrugging a bit self-consciously. "I just like to be prepared."

"How far does this preparation go?" she asked, half challenging, half joking.

He smiled in response. "Come in and see." He pushed the door open wide.

"Said the spider to the fly," she murmured, just loud enough for him to hear, earning a short masculine chuckle in return.

CHAPTER 13

Having his mate and child in his home was a wonderful feeling for Hank. He had never really had a chance to show off all the features he had been building into the structure over the past couple of years. Mark knew, of course, because Shelly was part of all the design work. She made sure that everyone who was building on the island had proper plans and triple checked calculations to make sure everything was done safely.

Other members of the Clan had specialized in engineering. Many worked side by side with Shelly, providing their expertise. There was more than one tunnel specialist because so many of the more resourceful Clan members had decided to excavate into the side of the caldera for their dens.

Hank, though, had probably taken it to the greatest extreme. He'd bored straight through the mountain, from the inner curve of the caldera to the outer mountainside. It wasn't something Mark encouraged many of his people to do, but if they followed specific guidelines, it was permissible in certain cases. Hank was interested to find out what Tracy would think of his escape hatch.

"This is really impressive," she said, walking into the wide hallway that led to the inner rooms of his home.

"We took advantage of the natural structure as much as

we could," he told her, leading the way. "It's still a work in progress," he said, opening a door to expose an empty section that didn't even have walls yet. "I put priority on my private quarters, office and the hatch."

"The what?" Tracy sounded intrigued.

"I'll show you, but maybe we should put Emma down first. I do have a spare room that we can make comfortable and safe for her," he assured her.

Emma was tired. All the excitement of the day had finally caught up with her, and Hank saw every indication that, once put to bed, the child would sleep for hours. Tracy nodded, and Hank led the way to the spare bedroom. It wasn't right next to his bedroom, but it was close enough, and he was already thinking about the surveillance gear in his office that he could repurpose to use as a baby monitor.

He knew he had an infrared camera with a motion sensor and mic pickup. That should suffice. He could rig it to his bedside monitors overnight, and they could keep tabs on Emma. They'd hear any sounds she made and be able to hear and see immediately if she made a move or had a bad dream. It would only take a few minutes to set up.

He escorted them to the spare room, opening the door and taking note of the duffel full of weapons he'd have to remove. He threw gear in here on occasion, but nothing other than the weapons satchel would pose a threat to Emma. There was a bed along one wall. It had originally been Hank's, but he had opted for a larger size when he built his bedroom.

He'd kept the old furniture, knowing he had a lot of space to fill in his lair. He'd kept it but had never had a guest here before, so it hadn't been used since he'd moved in. The room was clean though. He liked a tidy home and had a robot vacuum that made the rounds once a week whether he was here or not. He'd rigged it to self-empty into a waste chute he'd specially designed, so it never needed supervision.

"I've got bedding in this closet, and there's a bathroom through that door," he told Tracy, already opening the closet and taking out a set of clean white sheets, blankets and pillows. They'd make a little nest for Emma, and she'd be safe.

Tracy might possibly be thinking about sharing the room with their daughter. The bed was big enough for both of them. But Hank would be doing everything in his power to convince her to sleep in his bed. His *new* bed. With him. She just didn't know it yet.

Hank and Tracy worked well together as they tackled the tasks at hand. Tracy took Emma into the bathroom to wash up while Hank made the bed and quickly removed the weapons. He deposited them into his private office, grabbing the camera and being sure to lock the door behind him. If Emma did manage to wander around the house at some point unsupervised, he didn't want her getting into the weapons or his security equipment.

He'd installed the camera before Emma and Tracy came out of the bathroom. Then, it was time for sleepy hugs and baby kisses as they tucked their daughter into the improvised nest they'd created. Between one minute and the next, Emma had fallen into that deep sleep that he'd seen in other children of their species.

Hank and Tracy tiptoed out of the room and closed the door. He led her down the hall toward the hatch, wanting her to know everything about the place. So few people had been back here, he wanted to see her reaction.

"This is what I call my escape hatch," he said, entering a special code into a mechanical lock at the far end of the hall. It clicked, and he opened the door. Lights came on automatically and Tracy gasped when she saw what was inside.

"How in the world did you get that in here?" She stepped inside, motioning toward the small sea plane that had pride of place in the center of a large chamber that was essentially an airplane hangar.

"We have to winch it up after every use, but it's proven itself useful. I can launch from here, dropping down into the water, then motor out a ways before I take off. Mark's had me do it a few times when the island was under too much surveillance."

"I thought nobody came to the island without an invitation," Tracy said, tracing one hand along the body of the small plane.

"They don't, but Mark is a celebrity in both the human and shifter worlds. Especially in the early days, right after news of his purchase of the island hit the papers, we had a lot of unwanted attention from the paparazzi. They were circling the island in boats, helicopters, small planes, and even drones. It was a total pain in the ass for a while there, until we started fighting back."

"Fighting back?" Tracy looked at him sharply.

"Well, those drones are expensive and pretty easy to shoot down. Once Mark declared open season on them, we all got in a lot of target practice. It was kind of fun, actually," he mused with a grin. "The manned aircraft they buzzed us with stopped coming so close once they realized a lot of us crazy pilots would play chicken with them in the sky. And the island itself is defense against most watercraft. There's really only the one place to dock. Everywhere else is just too dangerous, filled with sharp rocks and other hazards—some of which, of course, we put there ourselves."

"Clever," she said softly, moving toward the front of the plane, which was facing outward toward the outside of the mountain. "So, you've got a retractable door here, like in some kind of superhero movie?"

"Yep," he told her, moving alongside and grinning as he looked at the giant door he'd helped install. "I figured if we were going to live inside a dormant volcano, we might as well go all the way." She shook her head, but she was smiling. "The doorway is carefully camouflaged from the outside. When we open it, we douse all the lights and roll the plane out. There's a gentle slope and then a sharp drop-off into the water. It's a hell of a ride, and gravity does all the work. We calculated the best spot to put this so that the prevailing winds and tides would carry the seaplane away from the island about ninety percent of the time, without having to engage the engines. This is a stealthy getaway special."

"Ingenious," Tracy murmured.

"I've got another surprise for you," Hank told her, bringing up the secure feed from the camera he'd put in Emma's room on his phone. He tilted it, so Tracy could see, then hit the sound icon that let them both hear their daughter's delicate breathing. "She's safe, and we can see and hear if she needs us."

"Do you have cameras all over?" Tracy sent a doubtful look around the large hangar.

Hank chuckled, pocketing his phone after one last glance at their sleeping baby. "No. I had that camera in my office, in a pile of components. I hooked it up just before you and Emma came out of the bathroom. I figured it would lend you some peace of mind should you decide to sleep…and maybe do other things…" he gave her a daring grin, one eyebrow raised, "…elsewhere."

"Just what sort of other things did you have in mind?" Playful. Interested. Hot. All good signs from his potential mate.

He tilted his head to one side, feeling mischievous. "Oh, a little of this, a little of that."

"Tell you what." She turned, putting both palms on his shoulders and stepping close. "Why don't we get on with the tour? I still haven't seen your bedroom." The invitation in her voice made his excitement level rise…among other things, as she sauntered away from him back toward the door.

He wasted no time closing and locking the door to the hangar behind them. He led her back down the hall, pointing to the door to his office, but not stopping, then opening the door to his bedroom with a flourish. He let her precede him inside, wondering what she'd think.

Tracy was enchanted by the large bedroom suite. She could see this was definitely Hank's inner sanctum, because it was decorated in a way that differed slightly from the rest of the house. Here, he seemed to have collected fabrics and mementos from his trips all around the world. There were hints of such things in other parts of the house. She'd noticed tribal drums displayed in the living room and colorful Italian glass on the open shelving in the kitchen, but this was more personal.

"You certainly are well traveled," she mused, walking slowly into the room.

Hank paused at her side while she looked around. "The masks were a gift from a friend in the African branch of the Kinkaid Clan," he told her, pointing to several lion-themed masks of natural wood and fibers in a primitive style. "The baskets are from my mother's extended family in South America."

"Let me guess," she said, moving farther into the big room. "The clocks are German." He had a small collection of miniature mantle clocks displayed on one dresser.

"My father came from a noble family in Austria," he said quietly. "The clocks are all that's left of his family's ancestral home, which was destroyed in the war. His great-great grandfather was a clock maker and collector. These were his pride and joy. My grandmother kept them safe and passed them down to my father, who left them to me."

"That's really nice," she said, running one finger along the edge of the dresser where the clocks were displayed. "You don't have them running? Do they work?"

"They do. I make sure to check them over every year, but the ticking drives me nuts," he admitted, making her chuckle.

She turned to find him right beside her. In fact, her little spin ended with her in his arms. Tricky. But she liked it.

"The bed has cotton sheets I picked up in Egypt. They're as soft as clouds," he promised, an anticipatory glitter in his sky-blue eyes.

"I may have to check that out," she replied, trying to sound serious when, in fact, all she wanted to do was jump his bones.

"I think that can be arranged, but first…" Hank took her hand and led her over to the nightstand where a small monitor sat, dark. He plugged it in, and the screen came to life, showing several images in a split screen of the outside areas around the house. He inputted a few commands, and the screen switched to showing a full image of the camera in Emma's room. Another touch on the screen brought up a light hum of ambient sound from that same camera. "We'll hear if she moves," he promised, setting the monitor back on the bedside table.

Tracy took a moment to check that her little girl was still sleeping comfortably. In fact, it didn't look like she'd moved at all from the position she'd been in when they left her. The day had been tiring for her, but exciting too. Emma showed every sign of enjoying her adventure—her first real trip away from Texas and the Big Wolf Pack.

Hank put his arms around Tracy's waist from behind and nuzzled her neck. "Now, where were we?"

She turned and put her arms around him, smiling up at him. "I think I was about to ravish you."

"You were?" He smiled in mock surprise. "I thought it was going to be the other way around."

She tilted her head, considering. "Well, maybe we could have a little of both?"

Hank's grin widened. "I like the way you think, sweetheart. I truly do."

They helped each other undress, kissing, licking and pausing now and again to push fabric out of the way and off, onto the floor. As they slow-danced their way ever closer to the bed, they left a trail of discarded clothing behind them, like a trail. By the time Hank lifted her up and lay her down on the bed, she was as naked as he, and her temperature was steadily rising into oblivion.

When he came down to lie beside her, she pounced on him. Her inner wolf was calling the shots now, and it had waited too long for the man it wanted. Tracy's human half wanted to slow things down…at least long enough to find a condom.

She must've said the word or maybe Hank was thinking along the same lines, because his arm flailed out to stab for the handle to the nightstand drawer. He latched it on the third try and pulled it open. Inside, Tracy saw a small box that looked new. It was still wrapped in clear plastic. She reached for the little box and began tearing at the uncooperative plastic. She growled as it resisted her fumbled attempts to pierce the slick outer shell of cellophane.

Hank chuckled as he reached out with one half-shifted claw and nicked it for her. Why hadn't she thought of that? She pushed the thought aside in her frenzy to get the rest of the flimsy barrier away from the paper of the box. Then, she was in, and there was more plastic and foil, but this time, she was happy to see it. She tore one of the little packets off and threw the box back on the nightstand.

Sliding down his body, Tracy held that single packet between her teeth, careful not to let her inner wolf elongate her canines into something that would render the prize within the little packet useless. She hadn't done this very often in her life, so it was both new and exciting as she tore open the little holder, then took Hank's hardness into her hands while she dressed him. Rolling that condom over his erection turned into an excuse to caress him, and she could tell she was turning him on even more as his hips levered up off the bed, into her caress.

She had to chuckle at his eagerness, though it matched her own. "Down, boy," she chided, giving him an extra squeeze as she licked her way back up his body. It had only been a short time, but she was already addicted to him. She wanted him more than she wanted her next breath. "I think this is the part where I ravish you," she told him, looking into his glowing eyes. Oh, yeah, her man was as excited as she was.

"I'm yours," he growled, spreading his arms out at his sides dramatically. "Do your worst."

A growl from her inner beast answered him as she rose above him, straddling his middle. She reached behind, finding his hardness, and lowered her body onto him, taking him in one long, slow stroke as his body vibrated with a low sound that could have been a purr.

When she was seated fully, she paused for a moment to savor. He felt so good. The perfect size and shape for her. He always had been. This was just part of the reason she'd been so unable to deny him back when they'd first hooked up, but it was a compelling one. She'd never been so compatible with another man physically...or emotionally. Her cat-man always seemed to know what she needed, and he'd been not only a generous lover, but a really good companion to a woman who had always been more lone wolf than Pack animal.

She began to ride him, slowly at first, then increasing in speed as her passions rose to overtake her. Hank's hands went to her hips, guiding her when she began to falter, her body moving in fits and jerks as a small orgasm took her.

He was still hard within her as he rolled them over and loomed deliciously above her. "I think this is where I get to ravish you," he told her, a loving smile on his face even as his body trembled slightly with peaked desire.

Then, he took over.

Hank rode her, this time, slamming into her in a way that made her feel his ultimate possession with an indescribably pleasure. He knew every place to touch her, every stroke that would drive her wild. In minutes, or maybe hours, she flew again, to a much higher place. A place she had only ever reached with him. Her Hank. Her lover. The father of her beloved child. The most special man she had ever known.

They came together, each rumbling a growl that probably would have been roars if they had been able to be as loud as they wanted. But it was all good. The beautiful reason they had to be quiet was fast asleep in the guest room and they would do what they had to do to make sure she was undisturbed.

Hank settled next to her, holding her close in his arms as they dozed. He took care of the condom, at some point, and rejoined her in the bed. They dozed for a bit, and Tracy was able to look over at the monitor to be certain her baby was all right in this strange new place.

They made love again in the deep of the night. This time, it was slow and seductive, Hank pulling out all the stops in his promised ravishment of her body. He was a beautiful man and a fantastic lover. He sent her to sleep with a lingering smile on her face that lasted well into the morning light.

CHAPTER 14

The next day, they ran into Pax and Ari Rojas in one of the community buildings that had just been completed. A sort of town hall, the design was both stunning and functional. Emma spotted the visiting brothers first, running over to them and demanding to be lifted in the air. Ari caught her as she launched herself at him and swung her up high, making her squeal in delight.

Tracy, who had charged after her runaway daughter, apologized. Only then, did she realize the brothers were accompanied by Mark and Shelly. Emma was probably interrupting an official tour or something, and Tracy felt even worse.

"I'm so sorry," she whispered to Shelly and Mark. "She seems to have no fear since she started shifting."

Mark gave her a solemn look. "That's the way I want all our children to be raised. You're a good parent that she feels so free to reach out to others."

"Don't worry," Shelly assured her as well. "We were just about wrapping up the tour, anyway. To be honest, I think we were boring them a bit, so a little play break is probably a good idea."

Tracy followed Shelly's gesture to find that both Pax and Ari were playing with Emma, tossing her from one to the other. It was only a short distance, and Emma seemed to instinctively know just how to twist her little body to land in the right position in each of the massive, outstretched arms.

"They won't drop her," Hank said, coming up beside her after shaking hands with Mark. "Look. She loves this game. And cats always land on their feet. See how she's twirling around, even in human form?"

"She's got good instincts. Good technique," Mark observed quietly to just their little group as they watched the game. "And, to be honest, I'm glad to see these guys are good with kids. If they come into the Clan, they're going to have to interact with everyone. Frankly, they're the biggest cats I've ever seen."

"Believe it or not, there are a couple of juveniles in Arizona that might end up a bit taller than these two. Apparently, a recent human ancestor was about seven feet tall, and his genes have bred true in subsequent generations. They say he came to their Clan from Samoa," Hank imparted.

"It boggles the mind," Mark said softly, grinning. "I'd like to meet more of these part-Samoan jaguars."

"If these two like you, they'll probably give the all clear to their leadership, and you might just get an invitation. Unlike most jaguar Clans, the Arizona cats are very involved with their extended families. They lost a lot of the males our age and older, so these two have become a sort of de facto team of betas, who vet everything for the Clan. Like Nick does for you," Hank explained.

"Sounds like you do something similar—vetting potential allies for your Clan," Tracy observed when Mark said nothing.

"Sometimes," Hank admitted. "When that's what's needed. Other times, I do whatever needs doing."

"Hank's one of the best troubleshooters we have," Mark put in. "I depend on him, as does the rest of the Clan."

High praise, indeed, Tracy well knew. Hank tried to play it down, but she could tell he was pleased with his Alpha's praise. Aside from the roles they played in the Clan, it was clear these two men had a deep friendship and respect that ran both ways.

"This is really different from Pack life," Tracy observed, speaking her thoughts aloud. "My dad is Alpha, and he doesn't really have casual friendships. Not like you guys. It's more of a totalitarian regime. At least, that's the term I used to jokingly use when I was a teen. It drove my dad crazy." Tracy chuckled at her own antics.

"From what I've observed, the Pack structure requires firm but fair leadership to be really successful. Like your father's Pack," Mark said, giving a nod to Tracy's dad's ability to lead. "We're a little different. We have an Alpha, to be the public face of the Clan, but we also have important people who play other roles. The Beta position is key—out of the limelight, the Beta is our protector, doing the research the Alpha needs to make important decisions and acting as counselor and co-leader in certain respects. Nick fills that role in our Clan, as the Rojas brothers do in their own. Our ancestors set up this system, hundreds of years ago, and it works for our people, but it's really not the same as a Pack. I don't rule absolutely," Mark told her. "I have a large support system, of which Hank is a crucial part."

Tracy grew even more impressed every time she learned more about the way the jaguars lived. It was the same in some ways, yet quite different to what she'd grown up with.

A jaguar kitten came streaking around the corner at full gallop. The baby wasn't too much bigger than Emma when she shifted. A few seconds later, a dark-haired man sprinted around the corner, chasing the youngster down. Both skidded to a halt in front of the Alpha pair.

Mark bent down to pick up the baby and cuddled him close. "Hey Mario," he said, addressing the older male who had been following the youngster. "This one giving you a run for your money?"

Mario laughed. "You bet. I saw him escaping from the nursery as I was walking past. Figured I'd help out by tracking him down and returning him to where he belongs."

Mark held the baby up to meet its intelligent gaze. "Miguel, I know you like to explore, but you're supposed to be with the others, right now."

A little kittenish yowl was his only answer, but Tracy thought the child looked maybe a little chagrinned at getting caught. Mark tossed the child to Mario, much like Pax and Ari had been tossing Emma in human form a few moments ago, and the cat-child twisted in the air like an old pro, to be caught easily by the other man.

"So, tossing children around is a thing among jaguars?" Tracy mused. Shelly laughed.

"You sort of get used to their antics after a while," the Alpha female assured Tracy. "Then again, I didn't grow up knowing about shifters and magic. This is all still kind of new to me, but I had a pet cat once."

The Alpha's muscular arm came around his mate's shoulders, hugging her to his side. "Are you comparing me with a house cat again?"

Shelly reached up and kissed her mate on the jaw. "If the shoe fits."

Mark growled and kissed his woman more thoroughly while Tracy smiled and looked away. It was clear to see how much in love the couple was. That boded well for their leadership of the entire Clan. When there was that much love at the top of the pecking order, it tended to filter down to every aspect of Pack life. Or Clan life, in this case.

Tracy's parents had been like that. While her mother had been alive, her father had been a very different man. He'd hardened a bit, since his mate's passing, but he'd always been a strong man. Most wouldn't have survived the loss of a mate, but the Pack had been in dire straits at the time, and they'd needed him so badly. As had Tracy. She'd been just a pup, and she thought maybe her father had stuck it out for her and for his people. Otherwise, he probably would have chosen to join her mother in the afterlife.

"Hey." Hank's voice was soft near her ear. "You okay?"

Smart cat to pick up on her change in mood. She looked

to see where Emma was and found her staring curiously at the jaguar child in Mario's arms. The furry baby was staring back at Emma, that same feline curiosity all over his fuzzy little face. Seeing her child roused Tracy out of her sad thoughts.

"I'm fine. Thanks." She put one hand on Hank's forearm, meaning so much in that simple word. "Do you think we can see the nursery Mario mentioned? Emma looks really eager to play with the other jaguar children. If that's okay..." Tracy looked first at Hank, then to the Alpha pair, who had stopped kissing and were paying attention to the conversation once more.

"Fine with me," Mark said graciously. "I think it would be good for your daughter to meet some other kids around her age. The school is nearby, and we have a fully qualified teaching staff who see to the education of the other kids, up through high school age. The nursery is there, too, staffed by various members of the Clan who are good with children. I'm sure they'd welcome Emma to playtime."

Mark's prediction was true, and Emma had a ball playing with the other kids while Hank took Tracy around to a few of the other community buildings—both those that had been finished and those under construction. He introduced her to a number of people, including little Miguel's parents, Julio and Leena.

Julio was the lead carpenter on the Clan home project and his mate, Leena, was a civil engineer who was acting as Project Manager. She wore a neon pink safety helmet that could be seen from a distance, and she welcomed Tracy with a big smile. Hank felt good watching the way the women interacted, talking about their kids and Leena telling Tracy about the amenities on the island and especially the school.

Julio's sister, Helena, was a teacher at the school, so the family probably knew more about it than most others. Hank was glad they were able to speak with Tracy and give her another parent's perspective on life for their child on the island.

When they picked up Emma at the nursery just before lunch, she was happy as a proverbial clam. Judy, a healer in the Clan who sometimes acted as the housekeeper up at the mansion, told them that they'd been working on having Emma learn to undress, at least partially, before shifting so she didn't ruin her clothing. That was a lesson Tracy had been trying to teach her baby but hadn't really known how to implement because wolf pups didn't generally shift until puberty.

"She shifted?" Hank asked.

"She did," Judy replied with a smile for Emma who was basking in all the attention. "And she remembered to loosen her clothes so they didn't get ruined." Judy patted the little girl's hair then shifted focus to Tracy. "She's a fast learner, and she was fine with the other kittens. I helped her get dressed when she was human again."

"Thank you so much," Tracy said, sounding grateful. "I haven't been able to get her to do that at home."

"Before you leave, you should sit in on one of the nursery sessions. We teach them all sorts of basic stuff. We've been dealing with baby shifters a long time, so we've developed a few tricks over the generations that usually work like a charm." Judy's smile was open and warm. There was a reason she was one of Hank's favorite people. She was a true sweetie.

"I'd like that. My kind don't shift this early, so it's been a real learning experience," Tracy admitted.

"I'll bet."

They chatted a bit longer about the children, and Tracy realized, yet again, that she had a lot to learn about little jaguars. She also understood how important it was for Emma to be around others like herself. That was something Tracy could fix. Hank was making it easy for her to do so. She just had to figure out where she stood with him before she decided just how involved she was going to allow herself to become with him.

Who was she kidding? She was already up to her eyeballs—and more interesting places—with him. But she still really needed to be sure this was the real deal before she could commit herself all the way to everything that being with Hank entailed.

Would she have to give up her Pack? How would that even work? How could she be the lone wolf among a Clan of jaguars? They all seemed welcoming enough now, but long term, could it really work? She just wasn't sure.

"If you want, you could bring Emma back for the afternoon session. *Abuela* is coming to tell stories of the Clan's history. She's very popular with all the children. Most of the adults too, actually," Judy invited. "We're happy to include Emma, and it'll give you a bit more freedom to explore the island."

"Thanks. I'm not sure what we're doing this afternoon, but if it works out, I'd like that. I'm sure Emma would, too." Tracy lifted her baby girl in her arms, and after a few moments where Emma said bye-bye to her new friends, they left the nursery.

Hank escorted them to another community building where a small crowd was gathering. "This is the dining hall. Everyone who's working on the building projects eats lunch here most days. I figured you wouldn't mind meeting more of the locals," Hank said with a wink, "and this way, we don't have to cook."

Hank led her through the cafeteria-style line where they made selections from a great buffet, then seated them at a large table that was soon filled to capacity. Tracy was introduced around. Most of the jaguars were younger than Hank, but she soon learned that though he was universally liked by every age group, the younger set had great admiration for his sense of humor and ingenious practical jokes.

Over the delicious meal, they regaled her with some of his more infamous antics. Like the time he put shaving cream in

Mark's boots then called a fire drill in the middle of the night. Apparently, Hank's willingness to prank even the Alpha cat made him a bit of a hero to the younger set.

They also seemed to love the time Hank had painted Nick's favorite security vehicle pink. It had taken stealth and a lot of pink spray paint, but he'd managed to do it three times in a row before the head of security caught him at it.

The chase that took place all over the island after that was apparently legendary. Both men had shifted, and the two jaguars were seen leaping from tree to stone to ground and doing things that even the other jaguars thought were impossible.

"Fear of losing a limb was a great motivator," Hank admitted with a chuckle. "Nick was threatening to rip my arm off, and he was mad enough that I was afraid he might follow through." They all laughed. "But it sure was funny watching him drive around the island in a pink Jeep for a few days at a time before he could get it repainted."

Tracy could just imagine the stoic head of security having to keep his chin up while parading around the green paradise in a hot pink vehicle. Too funny.

There was a common theme in all of the pranks they described that Hank had pulled. First, he never hurt anybody or destroyed their belongings. His pranks were not malicious in any way, and he always managed to make the person he targeted laugh...eventually. His humor was good-hearted, not mean-spirited. She liked that.

After lunch, they dropped Emma back at the nursery and resumed their tour. Hank took her around the perimeter of the designated public areas, so she could begin to learn some of the markers that denoted private territories. It wasn't certain, by any means, that she'd stay on the island, but Hank was applying pressure, both subtle and not-so-subtle.

If she could just have a little time to think. She was dealing with information overload and an emotional roller coaster at the same time. She had to slow down for a few minutes and clear her mind. A run would be really good, but she was almost afraid to go wolf on an island full of giant, predatory cats. Besides, the wolf acted on instinct. The woman was the thinker, and she needed a little space from the very distracting and disturbing presence of the man who wanted to be her mate, in order to do it.

"Would it be okay if I just walked around by myself for a bit?" Tracy asked Hank suddenly. He'd just finished their circumference of the public areas, so she knew the general layout of where the private territories began and felt safe enough if she stuck to the community paths.

Hank looked as if she'd struck him. She didn't need the added pressure, right now, of being responsible for his feelings, but she still felt guilty about putting that look on his face.

Darnit.

"I just need a little space," she went on, trying to soften her words. "A little time alone to think."

Hank stepped back from her, trying to hide his feelings, but her inner wolf felt she'd hurt him, somehow. Still, he backed off. He seemed reluctant but resigned, and she breathed a sigh of relief. She'd had a little too much togetherness for a woman used to living on her own since the birth of her daughter.

"Stick to the communal areas, and you'll be fine," he told her, backing away another step. "Do you know how to find the path to my territory?"

He'd only pointed it out like three times. Tracy rolled her eyes and nodded. "I can find your place. No problem," she assured him.

"I'll be in my office until just before the afternoon session at the nursery ends. You can find me at home, or meet me at the nursery then. Or, if you need more time, I'll just pick up Emma and bring her back to my place. We'll be there when you're ready."

She was glad he was being so reasonable about this, but she probably wouldn't need *that* much time. She was still a mom, and she still wanted to be there for her daughter.

"I won't be that long. I'll probably meet you at the nursery, and we can go on together from there." Surely, her ruminations wouldn't take so long she'd miss seeing Emma's excited little face after her day with the other cats and the Clan's grandmother.

She walked away from him first, slipping down the path toward the town hall somewhat aimlessly. She'd seen a sort of park space with benches around a tiny pond with a waterfall near the school. She would see if it was empty, and if so, she'd start off there. The sound of trickling water had always been peaceful to her. Maybe that and the lush, green surroundings would help her think.

Tracy was sitting on one of the benches when she heard someone walking nearby. Not a shifter, judging by the loud footsteps. There were few humans on the island, so it might very well be the Alpha female. Sure enough, a few moments later, Shelly came over to stand by Tracy's bench.

"Do you mind if I join you?" Shelly asked politely.

"Not at all." Truthfully, Tracy had been getting nowhere on her own. She was still as confused as ever.

Shelly smiled and took a seat. "Thinking weighty thoughts?" she asked after a moment's consideration of Tracy's expression.

"How'd you guess?" Tracy gave a short chuckle. No sense hiding the obvious and pretending everything was okay. Everybody knew she was the odd wolf out here and she had to make some important decisions where her child's future was concerned.

"You know, being one of the only humans here is a little tough sometimes. There are a lot of things I can't participate in with only two feet. The cats like to run and chase each other, and all I can do is watch and pray nobody gets too seriously hurt. But you're a shifter, so you have a lot more in common with everyone else than I do." Shelly jumped right in when she had something to say. Tracy could respect that.

"I might be a shifter, but a wolf Pack is a lot different from this, and it's not a picnic to be the only wolf in a sea of cats." Tracy paused, then went on with brutal honesty. "Just as it won't be easy for my baby to be the only cat in a wolf Pack."

"Would they chase her?" Shelly looked instantly concerned.

"Only if they want to get bitten by me," Tracy replied with a soft growl. Nobody would touch her baby.

Shelly started then laughed. "Oh, you have more in common with these jaguars than you think. Any other mother on the island would have given me the exact same reply."

"Motherhood makes us all a bit protective," Tracy mused with a smile.

"Humans get that way too," Shelly assured her. "You know, I do sympathize with your position. One way, you might be uncomfortable, the other way, your child could be. It's a tricky situation."

"I really don't know what to do," Tracy admitted. "I'd hoped getting away from Hank for a few moments might allow me to clear my head a bit."

"Yeah, these jaguar males are very distracting, aren't they?" Shelly gave Tracy a knowing smile. "Well, you've got space. What is your head telling you?"

"Nothing so far," Tracy admitted. "I'm still confused about what I should do."

"Then, what's your heart telling you?" Shelly asked softly.

"My heart?" Tracy was touched by the Alpha female's words. "My heart says to grab on to everything Hank is offering and keep it—keep him—for always. Not just for Emma's sake, but for my own, as well." Tracy only realized the deep truth behind her words once they were out in the open. Damn. Had she really allowed Hank so deep into her heart that she wanted to be with him always? But was that the wise thing to do? She still didn't know for sure. "Of course, that's a fantasy," she was quick to add. "I can have the Pack life I've always known, or I can jump into this jaguar existence that is totally alien to me, but will probably be better for my daughter."

Shelly looked at Tracy with a penetrating gaze. "Why can't you have both?"

"What?" Tracy shook her head. Had she really been thinking so all or nothing? Was it even possible to live both lives?

"Why can't you have both?" Shelly repeated firmly. "Hank's a pilot, and he owns a fleet of planes. He's rich. He can afford to fly you back and forth every other day if you wanted. Heck, he can teach you to fly, and you can do it yourself. Nothing says you have to pick either Pack or Clan. I know for certain because my mate has been talking to your father, and he says your dad is okay with you traveling back and forth. He's not going to disown you and Emma or anything. Heck, the last I heard, he was even talking about adopting Hank into your Pack and forming a strategic alliance."

"Seriously?" Tracy was caught flat footed by the Alpha female's knowledge.

Tracy's father hadn't said anything about that sort of thing to her. And the bit about Hank owning a fleet of airplanes and being rich? Tracy found it hard to reconcile with her knowledge of the man who had fathered her child. Then again, he'd been really casual about setting up that trust fund for Emma…

Tracy shook her head. Shelly rose to her feet and looked down at Tracy with a compassionate expression.

"I see I've given you a lot to think about." Shelly's words were kind, as was her smile. "I don't say this to many people, but in your case, Tracy, I really do think you *can* have it all. My advice, for what it's worth, is to give it a chance. Give Hank a chance. He's a good man, and I think he would make a devoted mate if you let him try."

Shelly walked away, saying no more. She left behind a stunned Tracy, but somehow, her words had helped make things clearer. The muddled thoughts that had plagued Tracy were starting to clear. She didn't have all the answers yet, but the lost feeling was dissipating, and she thought she had a plan on how to move forward. Maybe.

That thought firmly in mind, she left the park a short while later to meet up with Hank. It was almost time for the afternoon nursery session to let out, so she decided to meet him there.

CHAPTER 15

Hank was both pleased and relieved to find Tracy waiting for him when he arrived a little early outside the nursery. She'd taken a seat on one of the benches just outside the doorway, put there for exactly this purpose—to give those waiting to pick up children a place to wait. Nobody else was waiting yet, so they had the place to themselves, for now.

Hank walked right up to Tracy and stood silently, waiting to hear what she might have to say. She was so beautiful, his breath caught in his throat, as it usually did whenever he saw her. His inner cat was completely enchanted by her. He wanted to be with her, no matter what. The ball was in her court now. Their future depended on her decisions. He loved her too much to try to force her or con her in any way into staying, but he knew his heart would be torn asunder should she decide to go.

"Is it true that you own a fleet of airplanes?"

Now, that was a question he hadn't expected. Still, Tracy was a very intelligent woman, and also very observant. Plus, she was making friends on the island. No doubt, someone had seen fit to enlighten her about certain things.

Hank sat down next to her. "Fleet might be putting it a bit strongly. I do own a number of aircraft," he admitted, somewhat reluctantly.

He was never comfortable talking about the success he had found working for, and with, one of the most brilliant minds in the business sector today. Mark had been Hank's sounding board for various investments he'd made that had paid off handsomely. Mark was the kind of friend—the kind of leader—that encouraged everyone to succeed. He gave his advice freely and was genuinely happy when everyone did well.

"I know you had the means to set up the trust fund for Emma, but I didn't realize that was just the tip of the iceberg. You're a rich man, aren't you, Hank?" Her tone sounded accusatory to him, and he began to fidget a bit under her scrutiny.

"Does it matter?" he finally asked. "I'm nowhere near Mark's level, but I suppose I'm what my ancestors would've called a man of means. It's nice to have financial security, but making money isn't the sole purpose of my existence. When I didn't have any, life was simpler but a lot less stable. Having money means I don't have to worry—about that, at least."

Tracy seemed to weigh his words. "I guess I can understand that. But I'm still not sure why you kept it a secret from me. Were you worried I was only after your money?"

He hung his head. When he spoke, it was in a low voice.

"I have been hunted before—by human women, mostly—when they realized. I don't want that. Especially from you. I don't want to be wanted only for my fortune." It was a painful admission.

He looked up to see how Tracy had taken his words and was surprised to find compassion and understanding in her expression. Then again, he should have known she would understand. She was the daughter of a rich and powerful Alpha. Mating her would bring automatic prestige to a wolf of lower rank. Perhaps she'd had her share of pursuers, as well.

"To answer your question…no. It doesn't matter to me if you're a billionaire, millionaire, or you don't have two cents to rub together. I mean, it's good to know that Emma won't have problems with money if something ever happens to me, but I already knew that, because I have no doubt my father would provide for her, even if she isn't a wolf. So, she's secure in any case. As for myself, I like working and never had aspirations of living the high life." She chuckled. "Money is good to have, for the security aspect, but otherwise unimportant compared to other things."

"Other things like what?" Hank asked, intrigued.

"Things like honor and loyalty…and love," she said in a quiet way that was unlike her usual confident manner. They were getting to the heart of it now. "Hank, I… I understand why you wouldn't like to be wanted only for your money, because I… I don't want you to be with me only because of our daughter."

"Oh, Tracy…" Hank didn't have the words, so he moved closer and took her into his arms. "Tracy…" He placed little kisses on her hair, her brow, her cheeks. "I want you for *you*. Emma is a lovely bonus, but I was trying to get back to Texas all this time to see you, honey. That hasn't changed. I yearned for you all the time we were apart, and I was too stupid to realize you were my mate. My cat knew. It pined for you. It was my human side that just couldn't compute the idea of mating outside the feline species." He shook his head. "Stupid, I know. And I'm so sorry."

"Your jaguar thought I was your mate?" she asked, a flicker of hope in her pretty eyes.

Hank nodded solemnly. "I couldn't be with anyone else. In the years we were apart, I was never unfaithful to you. I had no interest in any other female, because you're mine. And I'm yours. I was just too stupid to see it." He looked deep into her eyes. "Can you ever forgive me? Can you trust that I'm telling you the gods-honest truth?"

She seemed to consider, then took a deep breath. "I will if you will."

Hank frowned. Did she mean…?

"I'll trust that you want me not just because of Emma, if you'll believe that I don't give a fig for your fortune. And, you need to forgive me for not telling you about Emma from the start. My only excuse was that I was scared…of so many unknown factors. I was afraid of your reaction—whether you'd want to take her from me. I was afraid of what my father might do to you. Of what the Pack might do. It was all too much, and it made me into a coward. I'm really sorry." She took a deep breath. "Maybe from here on, we can just trust each other and share the risk."

"There's no risk on my side," he told her gently. "I love you, Trace."

Her eyes widened, and he saw joy flash to life in their depths. "There's no risk on my side either because I love you too, Hank."

They kissed, their joy overflowing into the sweetest kiss he'd ever tasted. Tracy loved him. Tracy loved *him*!

He might just melt into the ground in happiness, but not before he kissed his mate a few more times…or a million more times…but who was counting?

*

The following days were the most blissful Hank had ever known. He and Tracy were learning their way together, ironing out what they planned to do. They both knew plans were always subject to change, but they found agreement on the big-picture items easily enough.

They'd decided to split their time between Texas and Jaguar Island. They would maintain homes in both places, though most of Emma's schooling—when it came time for proper education—would be done on the island, among cats. Tracy had spoken to the teachers and learned about the school curriculum. She'd investigated everything thoroughly before conceding that Emma would get a better education in a less stressful environment on the island.

She'd called her father and broken the news, inviting Hank into the conversation over his speakerphone once she was sure her father was okay with her mating a jaguar. Hank could've told her he'd already received the Alpha wolf's blessing, but he decided to let her find that out on her own. As it was, Joe Villalobos was very vocal in his congratulations and chided Hank as to what took him so long. They ended the call on a happy note, with a promise to be "home" soon.

Meanwhile, the Rojas twins had been making friends and learning all about the island. Hank sat down with them one night after dinner to talk. They wanted his take on the island setup, and he gave them the absolute truth, as he saw it. He had come to value the brothers' friendship. They'd been among the first to congratulate him and Tracy on their mating, and they'd taken due credit for helping get them together.

When Mark was notified, he immediately instigated a Clan-wide party to celebrate their union. Tracy seemed delighted with the consideration shown to her and their daughter by everyone, and Hank was just as flabbergasted by the massive party that went on from noon to well after midnight. He was also humbled by the outpouring of love from everyone on the island. He'd known he was a popular fellow because of his sense of humor, calm manner, and reputation for having been a practical joker as a younger man, but he'd had no idea his people cared so much about him, and his future happiness. It was an eye opener, in such a gratifying way.

Hank was about ninety percent certain that Pax and Ari would accept Mark's offer, but they weren't saying one way or the other until after they had spoken with their kin back in Arizona. About a week after they'd arrived, Hank had them all back on the plane, headed for the mainland.

When they landed in Texas, the Big Wolf Pack held a giant party to celebrate their mating. Pax and Ari were invited to attend and were a big hit with the single ladies of the wolf Pack. Now that they'd seen one successful mating between jaguar and wolf, it was *game on* for cross-species dating and fooling around. Pax and Ari were young enough to enjoy every minute of it.

Hank was just glad he had his mate and his child. It was something he'd searched for but never thought he'd find. He counted himself blessed by the Mother of All to have not only Tracy, but also Emma, in his life. He would live for them now, for the rest of his life, and he would be grateful every day.

He'd brought some of his things to keep at Tracy's house in Texas, which would now be *their* home, just as his lair on the island was also theirs. It was as he and Tracy were putting his things away—she making room in her closets for his hangers and emptying a couple of drawers in the dresser for his foldable clothes—that he took her in his arms and kissed her.

"What was that for?" she asked with a grin when he let her up for air.

"That," he said gently, stroking a stray curl back from her face, "was for being my true mate, the mother of my child, and my forever love."

He'd gotten better at expressing his feelings since they'd declared their love outside the school, but he'd never summed it all up as he'd just done. He was a bit dismayed to see tears fill Tracy's eyes. He'd expected her to be happy with his declarations.

"Should I have just kept my big mouth shut?" he wondered, feeling like he was on shaky ground. He was still very new at this mating thing, and he was bound to make mistakes.

"No," Tracy assured him. She reached up to cup his cheeks, a tear sliding down hers, even as she gave him a wobbly smile. "I just… I want you to know that I feel it too. We're true mates. This isn't just a convenience. It's not just because we made a baby together. This feeling… This is because I believe we were always meant to be. This is…forever."

*

A week later, after the big party at Big Wolf Lodge and Pax and Ari had been flown back to Arizona to deliberate with their Pack, Hank, Tracy and Emma were having a family dinner together in their house. Hank and Tracy had decided jointly to tell Emma about Hank's real role in her life. They hadn't said anything yet, not really knowing how much she understood.

She was a bright little girl, but she was still really just a baby, and she'd seemed to take the presence of Hank in her house in stride. She hadn't asked any questions, and Tracy decided it would probably be wise to find out what their daughter understood and what she thought about having Hank around all the time. She had broached the subject with Hank the night before, and he'd agreed.

Tracy took a deep breath, not sure how this was going to go. It could be a really important moment in their daughter's life...in their family's fledgling story.

"Emma, honey," Tracy began, trying to pry Emma's attention away from the peas she loved and was rolling around on her plate in a little game before she ate each one.

"Yes, Mama?" Emma looked up, though Tracy could tell she hadn't forgotten about the peas and her little game.

"I want to tell you something." Emma's attention span was better than most children her age, but Tracy knew she had to do this quick before she lost Emma to her peas again. "Mr. Hank is your daddy."

Emma looked back at her plate and started rolling another pea while Tracy's heart sank, but then, Emma said in a confident voice. "I know."

"You do?" Tracy and Hank spoke together, both sounding shocked by Emma's casual acceptance. Emma nodded, concentrating on her game, but still part of the conversation.

"How did you know, sweetie?" Tracy asked in a gentle tone.

Emma shrugged. "Cat knew."

Tracy looked at Hank, and he looked as astounded as she felt. "Your jaguar knew, honey?" Hank asked quietly. Emma nodded. "When did your jaguar know, Emma?" he followed up.

"First time," Emma told him innocently. "I saw you, Daddy." Emma looked up from her food, her eyes wide. "Okay Daddy now?"

Hank stood and scooped Emma into his arms, tears shining in his eyes. "Yes, munchkin," he told her, joy in his voice. "You can call me daddy or papa or father. And you're my baby girl."

Emma giggled and placed little baby kisses all over his face while Tracy's heart melted, never to be hardened again. Finally, they were complete. Though, Emma had been holding out on them. The thing Tracy had worried about—breaking the news to Emma that she had a real daddy—had been out there all along. They'd been a family all this time, but now, it was out in the open, for all the world to see.

The final bridge had been crossed, and Tracy's dearest secret was a secret no more. Her baby had her father, and Tracy finally had her true mate.

Life didn't get much sweeter than that.

# # #

ABOUT THE AUTHOR

Bianca D'Arc has run a laboratory, climbed the corporate ladder in the shark-infested streets of lower Manhattan, studied and taught martial arts, and earned the right to put a whole bunch of letters after her name, but she's always enjoyed writing more than any of her other pursuits. She grew up and still lives on Long Island, where she keeps busy with an extensive garden, several aquariums full of very demanding fish, and writing her favorite genres of paranormal, fantasy and sci-fi romance.

Bianca loves to hear from readers and can be reached through Twitter (@BiancaDArc), Facebook (BiancaDArcAuthor) or through the various links on her website.

WELCOME TO THE D'ARC SIDE…
WWW.BIANCADARC.COM

OTHER BOOKS BY BIANCA D'ARC

Gemini Project
Tag Team
Doubling Down

Guardians of the Dark
Half Past Dead
Once Bitten, Twice Dead
A Darker Shade of Dead
The Beast Within
Dead Alert

Dragon Knights
Daughters of the Dragon
Maiden Flight*
Border Lair
The Ice Dragon**
Prince of Spies***

Dragon Knights ~ Novellas
The Dragon Healer
Master at Arms
Wings of Change

Sons of Draconia
FireDrake
Dragon Storm
Keeper of the Flame
Hidden Dragons

The Sea Captain's Daughter
Book 1: Sea Dragon
Book 2: Dragon Fire
Book 3: Dragon Mates

Resonance Mates
Hara's Legacy**
Davin's Quest
Jaci's Experiment
Grady's Awakening
Harry's Sacrifice

StarLords
Hidden Talent
Talent For Trouble
Shy Talent

Jit'Suku Chronicles
Arcana
King of Swords
King of Cups
King of Clubs
King of Stars
End of the Line
Diva

In The Stars
The Cyborg Next Door
Heart of the Machine

Sons of Amber
Angel in the Badlands
Master of Her Heart

StarLords
Hidden Talent
Talent For Trouble
Shy Talent

Gifts of the Ancients
Warrior's Heart

WWW.BIANCADARC.COM